Where Light No Longer Shines

H. D. Pelton

Where Light No Longer Shines

H. D. Pelton

Mockingbird Lane Press

Mockingbird Lane Press—Maynard, Arkansas

ISBN: 978-1-64826-589-1

Library of Congress Control Number: Control Number is in publication data.

0 9 8 7 6 5 4 3 2 1

www.mockingbirdlanepress.com

Cover photo: H. D. Pelton
Cover graphics: Jamie Johnson

A legion of people helped me to this point. I could never name them all without leaving someone out. Above all, I must thank Paula, my wife. Without her encouragement, support, and patience nothing would be possible. My family for their belief that I could do this. I am also grateful for the early influence of Edgar Rice Burrows and Jack London. Their words were what sparked my interest in the author-built world. Dusty Richards, a friend and mentor I miss terribly. His books will forever be found on my bookshelf. He believed in my ability and helped me in so many ways. If not for him, I would have quit before I ever really got started. Friends like Floyd Keene, Rick Bratton, Rink Miller, and Jim Kane Sr. were some of my early readers. I must thank Regina Riney of Mockingbird Lane Press Publishing. It's nice when your editor, agent, and publisher is also a friend who can look you in the eye without blinking and tell you, "This ain't right. Fix it."

Dedicated to Paula. To whom I owe so much.

Prologue

October 1847. A bitter, wet presence floated its way under the heavy limbs of the black walnut tree. In the murky shadows, Patrick O'Brien felt the macabre presence snuggle close to his soul. It offered a whispered promise that smothered any resistance he might have had left. It joined the rotting-oak musk of fall.

Peace can be yours, came the seduction. *Peace—yes. And justice.*

Justice? Yes, he wanted justice. More than justice, he wanted peace. But wouldn't one bring the other?

Revenge. Revenge too, can be yours, came the delusion. *It will taste sweet.*

Revenge would be sweet—and he would find peace—he must find peace.

The ragged hole in your heart...I can fill it.

How many desperate sundowns had he endured now? How many soul-draining pints had his heart bled for his murdered son? How many times, at Helen's grave, had he prayed for solace? Only to endure silence.

What I require, is a simple thing.

Simple?

Kill him. That's all. You've killed before.

But that was a different kind of killing. That was for food.

Deer. Bear. Man. Killing is killing. Whether to right a wrong or for sustenance, it is no different.

Yes, Benjamin Ranklin deserved killing. His entire

1

life was nothing more than a long string of affronts. Every step of Ranklin's life washed him downstream, like a flash flood, toward this obvious end. Patrick would place Benjamin Ranklin's feet on the path to eternity. Then the dusky Reaper would gather Ben's soul into the fiery folds of hell. Benjamin Ranklin would be where he belonged. A homecoming long overdue.

You will taste your revenge. You will rejoice in your justice. You will have peace. All will be yours. And he... he will be mine.

The Specter snuggled closer, gripping Patrick's heart in its icy grip.

Such a simple thing, it cooed. *He deserves no less.* The voice reassured. *Did I mention closure?*

Patrick knew it was a lie. But it was a sweet lie. One he was ready to hear. The Ranklin clan had sliced Patrick's soul far too many times. They'd bled him with mental and physical wounds.

The cajoling voice kept whispering what Patrick wanted to hear. Each Ranklin male spawn was rotten to the core. Bad apples always spoiled the barrel. And the Ranklin barrel was full of black-hearted, rotten apples.

Each man of the Ranklin clan had committed his own specific crime against the O'Brien's. Each action cried for retribution. Until now, Patrick had faltered. Hesitating to be judge and executioner. Wasn't it best to leave it in God's hands?

Today that ended. No longer would he turn a deaf ear to the dark solicitor! Benjamin Ranklin deserved to attend the White Throne Judgement of God. He needed to answer for his sins.

The others would have to wait their turn. Forever

looking over their shoulders. Fearing the Reaper. Not knowing when their time would be up. Their hour of atonement would come. All in its own sweet time. But, for now—now it was Benjamin's turn. He would be the first.

There would be much *keening* from the Ranklin women. But all their wailing, blubbering, and tearing of hair wouldn't alter Benjamin's final destination one whit. Benjamin Ranklin would bust Hell wide open.

The time of O'Brien's grieving was over. This blood feud would now cut both ways. The shoe was on the other foot. There was no turning back. Patrick would do what needed doing and there would be no regrets.

A sudden gust of chilled wind skittered dead leaves across the gritty road. Like a nervous covey of quail running through a field before exploding into flight.

The specter snuggled closer.

1

Spring of 1833, the reality of the Arkansas Territory was not matching the visions Patrick's imagination had developed. He tugged at the neck of his plain shirt, desperate to get drier air inside.

Sitting stiff-backed on the plush, assistant pilot's bench of the steamboat *M. E. Parker's* pilothouse, he felt confined in the enclosure. Not because the space was small, which it wasn't by any means. It felt big enough to hold a dance. But because of the lack of air. A muggy, sticky oppression that matched his mood.

M. E. Parker was a beauty of a steamboat. Patrick hadn't had any problem picking her out among the clutter of vessels at the docks of New Orleans. Her gleaming white presence stood four decks tall and 175 feet long. She sported twin red-painted smokestacks with an American flag suspended between them. She had port and starboard paddle wheels covered with wooden covers. On these were boldly painted the name of the boat, *M. E. Parker,* in dark red paint trimmed in gold. On the top of it all, the crown itself was the Pilot House where he now uncomfortably sat.

The structure itself was the highest point of the boat. A sort of glass temple with a metal roof. Rectangular in shape, its wooden floor was covered in oilcloth. The sides were half wood on the lower section and the upper half was windows. A door punctured both port and starboard sides to facilitate exit and entry. A series of three windows could close out the weather from the front, but they were currently gapped wide open, held in place by small chains. There was a glass window behind Patrick and the sofa. That window didn't open. The side windows could be and were, raised as far as possible. Thin wooden sticks propped them up. Still, even with the spring breeze, the air pushing through felt sticky on the hairs of his forearm.

The windows sported red and gold curtains, pulled aside to allow 360° views. Rounding out the room's furnishings was a plush, leather chair sitting off to the side; a tabletop full of maps; two shiny brass cuspidors; a tall chair up front for the steersman; and a large stove for cold weather. Next to the starboard door stood a black man, a 'texas tender', with a white apron. Waiting for any requests from the captain for coffee or something from the galley. In the front of the pilothouse, lanyards for the whistle and a large bell dangled on each side of the ship's large steering wheel, or helm. Eight cylindrical spokes joined at a central hub made up the wheel. Its outer wooden hub inlaid with bright brass pieces was wrapped in fancy rope work. The spokes extended past the outer rim creating a series of handles the captain used to turn the wheel, thereby directing the boat. Other mechanical equipment included speaking-tubes to talk to the engine room, tiller rope and pedals. There was room enough for the captain to work from either side of the helm.

Here, high above the waterline, the pilothouse caught any breeze that was stirring. But it wasn't enough. Sweat collected under Patrick's brown felt bowler hat and trickled its way down through his reddish-brown hair. It slid down the back of his neck and pooled at the collar of his chocolate-colored work shirt. Even removing the bowler and fanning himself accomplished little. As a friend had once said, "It was as stifling as a South Carolina chicken coop in August."

Captain Hiram A. Clemens soaked up most of the incoming air. A large man, he stood in front of Patrick, just to the left of the helm, watching the river, one meaty hand gripping the large wheel while propping his right foot on one of its lower wooden spokes. From the tone of his rattling conversation, the humid air didn't affect him one bit. It was like he was a part of the river and all that it entailed. This was his world, and he ruled it.

With a little reflection, Patrick decided maybe his discomfort wasn't the humidity after all. It could be stupidity. His own.

Placing the bowler back on his head, he squinted hard to make out the next landing. Like the child's game of hide-n-seek, the landing seemed to dance and tease. Shapes appeared and disappeared in and out of the trees in the early morning mist. Under the thick forest canopy and behind the veil of thinning fog, Patrick could make out solid shapes lurking in the shadows. It might be buildings. It might be piles of driftwood. Then a blanket of thickening white obscured even the trees.

"Is that it?" he asked.

It was more pleading than a question. His stomach churned a little, threatening to empty its contents. What had the New York land speculator called it?

Land of Milk and Honey!

He'd known better.

Opportunity of a Lifetime!

How damn big a fool had he been?

Why you can stick a hoe handle in the ground at

sundown and in the morning, it'll be an apple tree budding with fruit!

No doubt the slick salesman had kissed the Blarney Stone, spinning tales no sensible man would believe. But his gifted tongue made the lies as easy to swallow as the Irish whiskey in Donovan's Pub.

And he'd damn sure swallowed plenty of both. He grabbed the offer in a double-fisted grip and pulled it close to his breast, the way a rummy would latch onto his last tankard of ale. Now, here he was—son and expecting wife in tow—halfway across a struggling continent—on a drunken impulse.

Opportunity or folly, there was no changing things now. What worried him most was that if things went bad, it wouldn't be him paying the price for his stupidity and pride. His family would suffer if this didn't turn out right. That bothered him.

Maybe those who ridiculed him back in County Cork had been right. Maybe he was nothing more than a drunk and a dreamer, infected with a bad case of wanderlust.

"That's her."

Captain Clemens' response brought him back to the present. The captain was squinting, but he was enjoying more success at boring a hole through the haze. A lifetime at the helm of a riverboat had its advantages. Twirling the ends of his handlebar mustache he pulled a calabash styled meerschaum pipe out of the corner of his mouth and used it as a pointer to stab at the fog draped riverbank a half-mile ahead.

"Right there she lays," he drawled. "On the lee side of that point. They call it 'Mouth of Arkansas' for lack of a better name."

7

Patrick ran nervous fingers through his reddish-brown hair, before jamming his bowler back on his head. It had been days since he'd taken a drink. A penance and a half-hearted promise that if all went well, he'd quit for good. His eyes were clear, but his nerves were raw. Once again, his stomach twitched, and he felt the familiar sour taste of whiskey percolate in the back of his throat.

"More name than the place deserves," he managed.

"Got to call it something," the captain tapped the latest edition of the navigator with the stem of his pipe, "to mark it on the charts."

Continuing to use the amber stem of the pipe as a pointer, the captain made a sweeping gesture with a plump right hand, encompassing all that lay outside.

Patrick followed with his gaze out the port window. The various shades of green from the sycamore, willow, and oak forest choking the riverbank mirrored those found on the opposite shore. The exception was a broad gap in the thick forest of the west bank. From underneath a dull, flint gray sky, a wet ribbon of yellowish water slid from the void. The light-colored current came well out into the big river before it blended with her gray-green flow. It put him in mind of the way Helen sometimes swirled cream into her tea.

"That'd be your Arkansas River," Clemens said. "She starts up in the Rockies. Near fifteen-hundred miles from here."

He checked his instruments before continuing.

"Picks up the Canadian, Cimarron, Neosho, and a handful more on her way down."

With a deep grunt, Clemens removed his foot from the wheel and moved closer to the open front of the Pilot

House. Shoving his face upward and using his broad nose, one that had smashed more than one fist over the years, he took a deep breath.

"From her look and smell," he concluded, "there's been a passel of rain up that way. Be a good thing if it holds steady."

The captain shifted and moved back to control the helm more firmly, placing a foot back on one of the wooden spokes, a frown wrinkling the corners of his eyes.

"It takes more water for the run between Little Rock and Fort Smith than it does from here to Little Rock." He nodded his head as if agreeing to his own summation. "Course that will increase the number of tree snags floating down and there's a danger there too." He shook his head from side to side and grunted out a small laugh.

"Ain't nothing easy about it either way you go. You always worry about the depth of the water. When I 'call for the lead', that means having a leadsman rush to the front of the boat and start throwing out a lead weight tied to a rope. He does that every hundred feet and tells me the depth of the water, and I can respond accordingly," the captain said. "Now, if he called out 2 foot, 10 feet, and so forth, especially in windy weather, I might not make out exactly what he was saying. Instead, we use our own river language."

"How so?"

"Well, if he calls out quarter less twain, that means the bottom is ten and one-half feet down," the captain said. "Mark twain means two fathoms or twelve feet. quarter twain is thirteen and one-half, half twain is fifteen feet and so on."

"I think I see."

9

"We can run at quarter less twain without much of a problem, but what I want to hear is no bottom!" the captain chuckled. "That means over twenty-four feet."

On each side of the boat, the *M. E. Parker's* double paddles chewed at the blending currents. Through the soles of his boots, Patrick could feel the steady rhythm of the steam engine three decks down on the boiler deck, a kind of half deck between the main deck and the Hurricane deck.

The vibration of its twin pistons, shifting back and forth, gave the boat the feel of a serpent undulating through the current. The constant, low hiss of leaking steam added to the sinister impression. Patrick was sure it was hissing something just to him.

It sounded a whole lot like *f-o-o-o-o-o-l.*

Reaching above his head, the captain jerked down hard on the lanyard attached to the boat's whistle.

Whoooooomp! Whoomp! Whoomp! Whooooooomp!

The brass instrument released a series of long, low pitched bawls of wet steam that bellowed across the water.

"Let 'em know we're coming."

The boat pushed closer to the area of slack water fronting the wilderness settlement. This would be the last stop before turning west. West—into the unknown. West—to a new life. West—to the end of the rainbow. West—to their destiny.

A shot of Irish whiskey sure would go down easy right now. Might even settle his stomach.

Drawing closer, structures became easier to pick out. Mouth of Arkansas, and the cluster of humanity that called it home existed on a whim. Even Patrick's untrained eye could see that. Perilously perched on a willow rimmed, low mound of silt between two major rivers, everything about it said temporary.

Shanty's that were little more than lean-to's, built of whatever material was at hand, were scattered across the puckered riverbank with no plan or design. Behind a hook-shaped bend in the Mississippi, the whole enterprise loafed slightly above the normal flow of the Arkansas. Under normal water conditions, the respective river eddies would cause little trouble. A rise of a few feet—from either river—it might cease to exist altogether.

The fog lifted higher, revealing a tangle of submerged trees. They created a barrier of sorts along the border between still water and strong current. Whole trees, uprooted by riverbank collapse, had floated downstream to be deposited when the current could no longer carry their water-soaked weight. This maze would have to be negotiated to accomplish a safe landing.

Bare, white, tree limbs resembling skeleton fingers reached out to grab any unsuspecting boatmen. But the submerged tree trunks, the resting place of soft-shell turtles, was where the real danger lay. One miscue by a captain and these jagged battering rams would tear the bottom out of a boat. The captain would have his work cut out for him.

"Have to ask you to leave the Pilot House now," Clemens apologized. "Gonna get a little busy in here."

Without looking at Patrick again, the captain started barking orders to his crew. "Call for the lead."

Leaving the captain to his work, Patrick made his way down past the luxurious staterooms of the Texas Deck, which was on the roof of the Hurricane Deck.

"No bottom," drifted from the front of the boat.

Patrick traveled down one more level to the Hurricane Deck, where the standard cabins were found. He couldn't afford the fancier staterooms of the Texas Deck, but the standard cabins weren't bad. After fetching his wife and child, maybe they'd go ashore to stretch their legs. That opportunity had only presented itself three times since leaving New Orleans.

Taking on firewood or picking up passengers was about the only reason to make a shore landing. The refueling stops were primary stops and they were well established. Loading firewood went quickly, not offering much time to go ashore.

If one of the secondary locations had potential passengers, or something needing shipping, they would run a flag up a pole, declaring they needed a boat to stop. With no flags flying to indicate potential passengers or profitable commerce, the *M. E. Parker* moved upriver with little wasted time. Dawdling cost the company time and money. Captain Clemens entertained no desire to waste either.

Patrick was halfway across the careworn, wooden deck of the *M. E. Parker's* Hurricane Deck when he felt a sudden shift in the deck beneath his feet. He'd been aboard long enough for his sea legs to take over and adjust automatically to the change. Still, he noticed it.

"Mark twain."

The boat broke free from the cross current from the Arkansas. The damp, earthy aroma floating on the breeze pushing across the face of the Arkansas River was overpowered and replaced with the unmistakable stench of rotting fish and stagnant water. Without looking, he knew they'd entered the slack water and were nearing the landing.

Reaching his cabin door, he tapped on the door jam. It wouldn't do to just barge in. He waited for Helen's reply. If the baby was asleep, flinging the door open would more than likely wake him. Then again, if Helen was in a state of undress, anyone strolling by could see right in. An open door didn't conceal much within the cramped confines of their 8 by 10 cabin. Unlike most of the women he'd encountered in this wilderness, Helen was modest and wouldn't appreciate the exposure.

A whispered, "come in," slipped from the other side of the cabin door. Figuring Connell was asleep, he tugged gently at the solid door. Bright light washed the interior, as the door swung open with a slight squeak of its metal hinges.

Helen was sitting in the only chair offered by the room. This disguised the fact that she was taller than her husband. After seven years of marriage, her natural beauty never failed to surprise him. A handsome woman, with an almond-shaped face and prominent cheekbones. She had a cupid's bow for an upper lip, which sat beneath a straight Greek nose. Wild, auburn hair framed and contrasted with bright, emerald-green eyes. The two-year-old son asleep in her arms only added to her beauty.

Connell's hair was red, like his mother's. Tucked behind rosy, cherub cheeks, he had his father's brown eyes. They were closed now, as a satisfied smile played across his face. When that happened, Helen said he was conversing with angels.

Caught in one of his rare quiet moments, Connell was sucking his left thumb while twisting curls of his mother's auburn hair around the fingers of his right hand.

"We're about to make a landing."

"Isn't this the last good one before we head up the Arkansas River?" Helen whispered.

Anticipation was evident in her voice. But she hadn't seen what passed for a good landing in this godforsaken territory.

"It is."

He reached out a calloused hand to stroke her freckled cheek. "But there's not much to it."

"That doesn't matter."

She moved Connell from her lap to her shoulder. The motion disturbed him and he began to stir. She stood, easing him down on the small, family shared cot and patted his bottom. The cherub's smile returned to his cheeks, exposing a dimple, and he headed back to sleep.

"It'd still be nice to walk around a bit," she said. "A person could go crazy looking at nothing but these four walls."

She'd been a real trooper; he'd have to admit. He could get out and visit with the captain and other men, but she'd been cooped up like a nesting hen. And the nest was tight. Filled with a steamer trunk, wrought iron cot, and one chair, it left little space for anything but sleeping or sitting. Throw a rambunctious two-year-old boy into the mix and everything shrank.

A shudder ran through the boat and its momentum shifted under them again. After days on the river, he automatically shuffled his feet to keep from losing his balance.

"Just reversed one of the paddle wheels."

"Then we're close," she said.

The noise level rose outside the cramped cabin as deckhands prepared for the landing and passengers made for the railings. The unexpected motion of the boat and the increased noise woke Connell. He started whimpering. Scooping him up from the cot, Patrick hugged his son close to his chest.

"How's me boy?"

Connell's frown sprang into a wide smile when he saw his father's beaming face. Patrick turned his back on the cabin and father and son stepped out the door to join the crowd. Patrick called over his shoulder to Helen.

"Come lass. Might as well see what I've gotten you into."

Taking a deep breath and warming her face with a pleasant smile, she joined her two men as they made their way to the railing. Gathered with the other passengers, they got their first look at the front door to their new home. The Arkansas Territory stared back with an indifferent, uncaring gaze.

Thomas Jefferson had opened this land with the Louisiana Purchase. Now President Jackson was saying it was the Nation's *manifest destiny* to fill it. This was their future. This would be their destiny.

2

The paddlewheeler danced a purposeful waltz, back and forth, dodging obstacles and lining itself up for the landfall. From their elevated lookout, the O'Brien's watched as the *M. E. Parker* finally nosed itself into the crumbling riverbank. The two heavy stages, wooden gangways used to load and unload passengers and cargo, were manhandled into place with a loud, wet smack. Guy lines, heavy ropes to hold the boat in place, were run to nearby trees. It took less than thirty minutes, as orders were shouted, and men jumped to respond. Like a stirred-up ant hill, it looked chaotic, but each ant knew their job and did it well.

Lost in the worker's performance, Patrick didn't immediately hear the deckhand walk up behind him. The sound of the man clearing his throat caught him a little off guard, but he recognized the man as soon as he turned around.

On those muggy nights when he'd had trouble sleeping, Patrick had prowled the ship. There was usually someone willing to put off some chore and chat with him for a while in the small hours of the night. This deckhand, in particular, seemed to take an interest in Patrick and his young family. He'd once told Patrick that *a hundred years ago*, he had left Ireland on an adventure to seek his fame and fortune in the big wide world. He'd found mighty little of either, he'd admitted with a twinkle in his one good eye.

"Aye, but I ain't quit looking," he'd cackled.

Patrick found no malice in this Irish runaway who was now grinning politely at them. The man stood with his head tilted slightly to the right, while his stringy beard pointed unapologetically left. A cotton, calico bandana tied over the crown of his head was doing yeoman's work keeping his greasy, gray hair under control while covering his bad eye. Patrick couldn't recall if he'd ever heard the man's name.

"Plan on going ashore, are ye?"

The deckhand continued to grin at Patrick and in a suddenly remembered show of proper manners; he tipped an imaginary hat to Helen.

"Be careful if I's you."

"What do you mean?" Patrick demanded.

"Keep a weather eye on what's valuable to you, I would."

The overgrown leprechaun again tipped his imaginary hat at Helen and with a slight bow, his hands outstretched to his sides, he backed away from the three. "Every man's his own law hereabouts," he cautioned. His impish grim seemed to grow wider. Turning on his heels, he made his way toward the ladder which led down to the main deck. He was quickly lost in the swirling mass of humanity.

"What strange advice," Patrick said.

A shout arose from below as people surged for the gangways and headed ashore. He quickly forgot the encounter in the desire to feel his land legs under him once again.

"What say we make for shore?" he said.

"Do you have coins?" Helen asked. "In case we find

something we need."

"That's not likely in this backwater."

His hand instinctively moved to the leather pouch suspended at his waist. On the way, his palm brushed across the staghorn handle of the 14-inch dirk hidden under his coat.

"Not unless you need partly tanned hides or rot-gut whiskey," he laughed. "But I've got coins in me money pouch if you decide you need either."

A lighthearted smile flashed across his face. "And if I need to 'protect me valuables', I've got me knife."

Helen's laugh tinkled like crystal in the muggy air. He could still remember the first time he'd heard it. To look at her beautiful face and feel that laughter sparkle its way up his spine, made him know anything was possible. It even made him forget his doubts—at least for a second. One glance ashore, however, and the doubts returned.

Helen took Connell's pudgy little hand and together the three made their way down the steps to the lower level. There they joined the procession moving ashore. Off to the side, work gangs respectfully waited for the exodus to subside before beginning the process of taking on firewood. At the head of the gangplank, Patrick took in the landing with a sweeping glance.

"Distant hills are not always greener," he volunteered. Sweeping his hat from his head, he wiped sweat from his forehead with his shirt sleeve. If he didn't look directly into Helen's eyes, maybe she wouldn't see how worried he really was.

"These are not *our* distant hills," she said. "We've still a way to go."

From one of the upper decks, the voice of Captain

Clemens boomed out the name of his first mate.

"Mr. Lewis!"

"Aye, sir?"

The soot-dusted first mate stopped what he was doing long enough to peer up at the bridge. "I'll not tolerate green wood, Mr. Lewis."

The loud conversation caused Patrick to turn his eyes up at the captain, as did a number of those on shore.

Clemens was standing at the railing of the Hurricane Deck, in full splendor. A real riverboat captain. Dressed in full length, double-breasted frock coat, neatly closed with large, gold buttons; gold trim at his cuffs; a leather Greek mariners cap squarely on his frosted head and hands on his hips. He looked every inch the man in charge. His booming voice carried clearly over the water and up the bank. It appeared he was directing his instructions to someone hiding onshore more so than to his first mate.

"Last trip, we were sold green wood at this landing!" His mustache whipped violently as he shouted the words. "Can't get any heat out of green wood, Mr. Lewis! A man who sells me green wood is doing his best to rob me, Mr. Lewis! Make sure it's well seasoned!"

"Aye, aye, sir," Lewis turned back to the waiting deckhands. "You heard the captain," he shouted. "Heave too and be quick about it!"

Patrick stooped to pick up his son as he moved down the gangplank. Connell giggled and twisted away. He'd been hiding behind his mother, while the captain's show was in progress, hanging on to the tail of her dress. Here was his chance to unlimber his chubby legs in a race down the wooden escape route to shore and to freedom.

But Patrick was quicker. He grabbed Connell under

his arms and swung the boy high into the air in a circular arch that ended with Connell settled happily on his father's shoulders. The boy squealed with delight. From his perch on his father's broad shoulders, Connell, grinning from ear to ear, was king of all he surveyed.

Helen brushed a wayward strand of red hair from her eyes and smiled as she slid her delicate hand into the crook of her husband's arm. She knew him better than he would like to admit. Usually, he was confident, sure of himself and his ability. That was the side he wanted her to know. This vulnerable side was something he didn't want her to see, so she would act like she didn't.

As she moved closer, he felt her warmth. Her lean and well-proportioned body wore the simple, homemade day dress like a ball gown. Only the keenest eye would have detected the slight bulge in her waistline indicating new life would soon enter the world.

Their shoes slipped a little on the sticky footpath as they wound their way up through the haphazard stacks of hardwood. Patrick hesitated and stepping to the side of the well-worn path, he drew his wife and child over with him. He turned toward the boat; his face captured in a faraway gaze. It was not the boat or even the river he was seeing, but the events that had led him to this place. He saw past the white-washed mass of the *M. E. Parker*—out past the bend, covered in river birch and willows. He looked past New Orleans—past the trip around Florida— all the way back to New York—and beyond to Ireland.

"Less road in front," he said, "than behind us."

"We've come a long way," Helen agreed with a sigh. "And we've left a lot behind."

She tried to hide the quiver in her voice, but he saw

the goosebumps dance on her bare forearms. Somebody just walked on her grave, his father would have said. Helen squared her shoulders as if resolving herself to some greater truth. She took a deep breath and continued, "We just need to leave it behind us."

"Some things are harder to leave than others."

He ran the course of events through his mind. Shortly after they'd married, he'd decided they needed to travel to America in search of a better life. A hard decision, true, leaving everything they knew. But he had hope.

They'd left the emerald hills of their ancient homeland and found themselves plunged into the filth of the slums of the Five Points district of New York. There they lost three children. Two to childbed fever and one to pneumonia just two short months after coming into this world. He'd nearly lost Helen to childbed fever too. When things were at their darkest, the God he thought had abandoned him blessed them with Connell. Before Connell's second birthday, Helen was expecting again.

The Five Points was a cold, hard place, lacking in all aspects of human decency. A place of disease, murder, and prostitution. Even after changing his Irish name from O'Bierne to O'Brien, he found steady employment an unattainable dream. A skilled craftsman, he should have been in demand. No one in New York wanted to hire a *Paddy*. Desperate for anything to improve his young family's situation, he had been easy pickings for the land speculator.

The new Arkansas Territory. Land of milk and honey. No worry about Indians. A place where a man could stick a hoe handle in the ground, and it would sprout into an apple tree overnight. You'd best take the offer now before someone beats you to your paradise.

He'd jumped at the chance. A lifeline to a drowning man. Through the haze of too much whiskey and too few prospects, he took the last of their savings and grabbed the offer with both hands. He purchased the land and then the equipment needed to start his own sawmill, without his usual consultation with Helen. Even with this slight, she'd stood firmly beside him, supporting her husband as always. Common sense and self-preservation would have overcome a lesser spirit.

But what if he was wrong...again? Perhaps the leprechaun had tricked him one too many times. Why did he think things would be better just over *this* next hill? How much more could his wife take? What would be the cost to his family? The answer to all his questions and doubts was drawing near. With a forced smile, he turned to Helen.

"We've got a couple of hours to fritter away," he said. "Let's see if we can find you a trading post of some sort."

Together they stepped back onto the well-worn path and headed into the deeper shade of the settlement. The path wound a circuitous route through the uneven stacks of wood and along the edge of a stagnant swamp. Cypress knees stabbed up through the brackish water clawing for a breath of air. Black clouds of mosquitoes patrolled what little air current dared stir in the deep shadows as water snakes glided across the surface of the tea-stained water. Mangy hounds lay here and there, too lazy to even growl.

Scattered cook fires bled a slimy film of smoke into the mix. It hung low, slightly above head height, and just stayed there, defiantly refusing to rise or to dissipate. Like the inhabitants of Mouth of Arkansas, the smoke seemed exhausted, unable and unwilling to muster the energy to fight its way up through the dense canopy of leaves. Everything about the place seemed to be in decline. Even the thrown together shacks appeared to be rotting down before the builders finished putting them up.

The arrival of the steamboat had attracted the attention of many of the area's human denizens. As the O'Brien's made their way to the center of the settlement, they passed small knots of hard-looking men and used up women. Some were moving in the general direction of the landing, either to transact some business or to see what was taking place on their front door. The human flotsam and jetsam of the river society darted suspicion and distrusting glances their way, but offered no friendly greetings, just an occasional guarded nod of the head.

Some of the more energetic men were gathering at the top of the riverbank, near the stacks of wood, where they could lean against trees, or sit on the ground, and observe the black deckhands working. Seemingly content with the free entertainment, they scratched and glared as the black men marched single file in a continuous circle.

The slaves glided off the boat onto shore, where the sticky mud squished up between their black toes with each step. Then up the bank to the stacks of wood, where they would hold out both arms at waist height. Other men would then load the large sticks of oak into their waiting arms, while the seller kept count. Each heavy stick elicited an involuntary grunt from the recipient. With sweat glistening on the bunched muscles of their bare backs, they would slip and slide back downhill and board the ship by the second stage. Here another group of slaves would remove the cargo and stack it neatly on the Main Deck near the furnace, behind the main staircase. Then off the human pack mules would go again, repeating the monotonous task. All the while, the slaves sang a mournful tune to keep time with the work. It seemed to fit the deadened outlook of their lives.

"Gotta watch 'em every minute," one grimy inhabitant of Mouth of Arkansas slurred.

"They'll steal anything whut ain't nailed down," came the reply.

"That's the gospel," added another.

A quick look around and Patrick wondered what would possibly be worth stealing here. Definitely not the half-submerged *currach* down at the swamp's edge. He thought they called them canoes hereabouts. A wood frame boat covered in tree bark instead of the traditional Irish currach covered with skins. Maybe they were afraid someone would take one of their pet water moccasins or perhaps that sickening stew he smelled scorching over a campfire. It was more likely that the riff-raff of Mouth of Arkansas were the ones looking for something to steal.

"I guess this passes for entertainment in the Purchase," he said. "Watching someone else work."

Helen placed her hand over her mouth to whisper her response. "What else have they got to do?"

She nodded in the direction of a man wearing a pair of overalls, just one strap over his shoulder, the other dangling loosely around his knee. It was the only piece of clothing keeping him from being as naked as God created him. He did offer a toothless grin as he swatted flies away from his scraggly beard.

"They sure don't waste time with baths or with shaving," she said.

Coming ashore with his wife and child might not have been such a good idea after all. A quick check with his right hand confirmed the dirk was still handy.

Seeing the subtle movement, Helen tried to lighten her husband's dark mood. She poked him in the ribs with her elbow and whispered, "I think you'll fit right in." Her smile used her whole face. It never failed to warm his soul. He rose to the bait.

"I'd look good in a beard."

He jutted his lower jaw out and twisted slightly to one side. He strained to look up at Connell still perched on his shoulders. "What'd you think me boy-o? Papa needs to grow a beard?"

Connell giggled, so Patrick dug his fingertips into the boy's ribs. The youngster giggled louder and clung even tighter to his perch. On this lighter note, they headed deeper into the makeshift community. Patrick's eyes still swept ahead, alert for danger. There was something sinister lurking in the shadows. The hair on the back of his neck told him so.

3

Two pairs of hooded, black eyes watched the young couple leave the steamboat and stroll toward the trading post.

"Ain't that a fine-looking filly!" Jacob Ranklin nearly slobbered, watching Helen walking with her husband and child.

Jacob Ranklin could be described as a bear ready to hibernate. He was slow, sluggish and fat. Those were his good features. Long, black, stringy hair did its best to hide his oversized ears. A stained and torn calico shirt covered his upper body, while wool pants with large grease stains draped loosely over his stumpy legs. Both pieces of clothing smelled of wood smoke and dried sweat. Jacob's eyes were dark, the skin below, puffy and pink. Dried in the corners of his mouth were nasty signs of tobacco use.

All of that, combined with a bulbous nose, made him look somewhat piggish.

"Get your mind back on business," growled his older brother, Benjamin.

Benjamin Ranklin was an entirely different creature. One surer of himself and more dangerous. If Jacob could be compared to a bear, it would be a black bear. Benjamin was a grizzly. Dressed in furs and skins, he looked the part of a mountain man. Long, black hair poured from under a cap of coyote fur. A coal-black beard hid his face, except where his over-sized nose resided. A trait he shared with his younger brother. He too used tobacco, but instead of snuff, he liked twist tobacco. Wandering bits of the clipped leaves decorated his beard. In moccasin feet, Benjamin Ranklin stood six-foot-two. Built like a powder keg, his disposition could be just as explosive.

Although the older Ranklin seemed to find fault with his younger brother leering at this female, Jacob noticed that he took a good, long look at the woman's retreating ramrod straight back and pleasantly round backside. When you found a female that easy on the eyes, you didn't squander the opportunity to look, especially this far from civilized society.

Jacob frowned and opened his mouth as if he was about to say something questioning why it was okay for Benjamin to look and not him. Thinking better of smarting off to his older brother, he clamped his mouth shut, with a pop that would have made a snapping turtle proud.

"You don't see many handsome women like that out here," he offered instead. "Hope this steamer is going at least up to Spadra Landing, and I hope she's riding it all the way."

"We been waiting seven days for the proper boat," Benjamin said. "If this is that boat, they'll be time on the river to sniff around after that."

"You traveled up this river a bunch when you traded with the Injuns," Jacob said. "How'd you get all your stuff upriver back then? I mean all those iron hatchets, mirrors, bolts of cloth, and such. That had to be hard. Did you take a steamboat then?"

"Hell no, you idiot," Benjamin spit the words out. "Weren't no damn steamboats on this river back then."

Jacob sullied like a possum at the rebuke.

"We had to paddle upriver in voyaging canoes," Benjamin's voice softened a little when he noticed the hurt on his brother's face. "You can get a lot of stuff in a good canoe and still handle it pretty good," he continued. "Then we'd build rafts to bring the furs back down to New Orleans. Then bust 'em apart and sell the lumber, then back we'd go again for another season."

"How far up did you go?"

"All the way to where the Arkansas is just a trickle."

"What traded best," Jacob asked. "Iron or cloth?"

"Whiskey was best," Ben laughed. "Nothing out trades whiskey. And it needn't be good stuff either."

"Who'd you like trading with the most?"

"The Cherokee and Osage could be cheated pretty easy with the lubrication of whiskey," Benjamin smiled at the remembrance. "It was a profitable enterprise back then."

"Speaking of profitable," Jacob sneered as he stared again in the direction the attractive woman had gone. "Let's hope it can be fun too."

"Let's go talk with the first mate," Benjamin jerked a thumb in the direction of the steamboat. "See about loading our plunder now." He shot his brother a wicked grin and winked a soulless eye. "Fun comes after."

Standing slowly, the older Ranklin scratched at some itch beneath his buckskin pants and stretched as if waking from a long nap. He then headed in the general direction of the river, toward the activity taking place at the boat. The younger brother fell in behind like a trailing puppy.

Picking out the first mate was an easy thing. Benjamin had him pegged long before they reached the riverbank. He stood on top of a large bundle of building supplies, on the Main Deck between the two gangways, cussing and pointing, lording his position of power. In general, he was just being an ass.

A long line of blacks shuffled off the boat on one gangplank, and back aboard by a second gangplank. Some were carrying armloads of wood, which they stacked on the lower deck near the boiler before heading back ashore, repeating the process all over again. Others were carrying various packages aboard. While still others used the overhead booms to load larger and heavier packets. As they worked, they all hummed a song to keep the rhythm of the work steady. It was apparent that the first mate thought his verbal supervision was what was keeping the ballet organized. His cursing was more of a fly in the ointment, causing more harm than good.

Every so often the first mate would be interrupted to barter a deal with a customer wanting to go upriver. When that happened, he had a hard time balancing his end of the conversation with his cussing of the blacks. Sometimes the freight paying passengers thought he was cussing them. They quickly let him know that they didn't appreciate it.

"You there, tote that forward—that goes aft—damn it!" he shouted. "Have you got no sense a'tall? Ferdinand! You know'd better'n that! Yes, sir? You want to go upriver? How far?"

"Little Rock."

"I'll skin your damn hide!"

"You talking to me?"

"No sir, not you. I's talking to that lazy black."

"Well, I won't stand for it."

"Get that wood loaded—keep it moving—we ain't got

all day. That'll be five dollars, sir."

"Seems a little high, but here it is."

"Damn it, Ferdinand!"

"If you're cussing me..."

"And thank you, sir."

"That's better."

"Get that idiot away from there—sorry, sir. No not you, sir."

Each group of men lined up for their opportunity to strike a deal with the first mate about themselves and whatever provisions they needed to load aboard. Immigrants, trappers, and regular river traffic had all collected at Mouth of Arkansas waiting for the chance to move up or down the Mississippi River or to head into the Arkansas Territory. Those wanting to head up the Arkansas seemed to have a sense of urgency, but for the most part, they waited patiently for their turn. Surely the boat wouldn't leave without them if there was room aboard and money to be made. Those who had already reached their agreement with the first mate began pointing out their respective piles and bundles to deckhands explaining what they needed loaded and which piles were theirs.

One immigrant with a heavy German accent was talking to the first mate about some bundles of roots of some kind. Something about the special care they must have. They needed to be loaded on top and not under something heavy.

The captain stepped out of the pilothouse again and, from the front of the Hurricane Deck, called down to the first mate below. "Store that stuff properly, Mr. Lewis."

"Aye, sir." The first mate didn't even bother to look

up.

"We've quite a bit to load, captain," he shouted back. "But it's coming along."

"Can't make money tied to the bank, Mr. Lewis."

"Aye, aye, sir."

Benjamin Ranklin eased nearer to the first mate, cold eyes watching for his chance.

"I want to talk to this huckleberry alone," he whispered to Jacob. "No need to haggle price with a bunch of greenhorns hanging on every word. They'd be comparing our deal with their own."

"Makes sense."

"An extra coin or two slipped slyly into his itchy fist, could make the price we pay melt some," he scratched at his beard. "Fare for our supplies, the growed-ups and your passel of young-uns could run into a handsome sum otherwise."

The two brothers watched for their chance as the German walked away.

"If this mate is of the normal stripe," Benjamin said as they eased nearer, "he'll bribe."

"You do the talking," the younger man agreed. "You know his breed."

4

The worn trail finally deposited the O'Brien's in the center of the settlement. Three good sized shacks crouched around a forty-yard-wide, semi-flat area free of grass and pocked with mud holes. A sow with a litter of squealing shoats was enjoying a soak in the deepest and blackest mud hole available.

A quick survey of the situation and Patrick selected the structure which seemed more solid than its neighbors. He figured it to be the main building since it didn't lean quite as bad as most. It was also the first shack he'd seen that didn't have a dirt floor. There was a small porch, which led to an open doorway. Above the dark void was a scrap of wood with a hand-written sign done in red paint. It simply stated "Post."

Swinging Connell down from his shoulders, Patrick placed the toddler's bare feet on the rough-hewn porch. A buffalo hide door was tied back to allow light, flies, and customers inside. Patrick cautiously entered the low structure, followed close by Connell then Helen. Immediately he was engulfed in the stink of freshly scraped beaver hides, salty pickle brine, dried sweat, and musky tobacco all bound together with a strong base of alcohol. Cracks in the walls, where the boards didn't quite meet, helped the bear oil lamps light the interior of the room. An open ceiling of peeled, gum tree post for rafters gave the impression of more height. From the poles hung traps, ropes, smoked meat, and thin, tattered strips of bark, giving fat horseflies a comfortable place to rest and regain their strength before their next attack.

"Are all river posts this rundown?" Helen whispered.

Patrick smiled and whispered back, "You mean the town or the people?"

Helen smiled and crossed the room to check out a table stacked high with bolts of calico cloth. A rail-thin man wearing a dirty apron looked up from behind a makeshift counter of planks stretched from top to top on two hardtack cracker barrels.

"Welcome," he said. "Welcome. My name is Jonas. Jonas Napoleon. I'm the proprietor of this fine establishment. How may I be of service?"

"Just looking around if you don't mind," Patrick said. "Arrived with the steamboat and wanted to get our land legs back."

"Looking is the cheap part. So, look to your heart's content. Everything's for sale or trade, including the building." Jonas laughed at his own joke.

"Thank you."

"That's a good-looking boy you got there," Jonas smiled. "Wanna trade him?"

Connell quickly slipped behind his mother, grabbing hold of her dress tail. From his sanctuary, he peered shyly around at the stranger.

"What you got to offer," Patrick played the man's game.

"I got a broke down old hound around here somewhere," Jonas was enjoying the exchange. "Ain't caught a rabbit in years. All he does is eat and sleep."

"I can't see where either of us would be improving our situation," Patrick reached out and tousled Connell's hair.

"That's all this 'un does. Guess I'll keep him for now."

Jonas laughed out loud. A strong, full-bodied laugh that filled the small building.

"Tell you what I'll do," he continued. "I'll sweeten the deal with a peppermint." Picking up a glass jar from the countertop, Jonas removed the lid and offered its sweet contents toward Connell. "If'n your momma don't mind."

Jonas and Connell both gave a quick look for approval to Helen.

"That's awfully kind of you, sir," she said. "But not necessary."

"If'n it was necessary, I'd probably do it grudgingly," Jonas smiled. "But when it comes to young'un's, it's a definite pleasure."

Connell looked up at his mother. It was obvious he wanted the candy, but he was still unsure of this loud stranger.

"Go ahead," she said. "You may have one piece, but no more. And tell Mr. Napoleon, thank you."

Connell eased around his mother, keeping a firm grasp on her dress with one hand. He reached out and took the offered treat, then quickly returned to his sanctuary.

"Tank u," he said as he retreated.

"That's a fine young man you've got there," Jonas said as he straightened back up. "Got more manners than most grown folks." Placing the glass jar back among the clutter on the countertop, Jonas turned to the other strong suit of a true salesman—gossip.

"Where you folks headed?"

"Going upriver to Spadra Landing," Patrick replied. "We've bought some land up that way."

34

"Seems to be a popular place," Jonas said. "I know of two other families here headed that way."

"We'd be interested in meeting them," Patrick said. "If you could tell us who they are."

"The Göbel's is one. They're a couple about your age. Only the two of 'em," Jonas said. "From Germany, if I remember right. Nice folks. No children though. You'll recognize 'em right off. He's tall and square-built. Always fussing with some grape stock, he 'brought from the Old Country.' Claims he's gonna make wine. Name's Hans. The wife, Elizabeth, she's taller than most and solid built. A handsome woman to be sure." He quickly added, "But not as handsome as yourself, if you'll pardon my boldness ma'am."

"What about the others you mentioned?" Helen's cheeks flushed as she tried to gloss over the compliment.

"That'd be the Ranklin's," a frown clouded Jonas' narrow face. "A mean-spirited bunch. Two brothers. One much older. Goes by the name of Benjamin. Younger brother named Jacob. Both got wives. Can't say I ever heard the wives' names though. Jacob, now he got a passel of kids. Ain't a sign of manners in the whole litter."

"How will we recognize them?" Patrick asked.

"You'll have no trouble recognizing them." Jonas shook his head. "Both got eyes as black as their souls. I'd keep my distance if'n I was you."

"I'll give them a fair shake," Patrick said. "I'll not judge them until I get to know them."

"Fore-warned is fore-armed," Jonas proclaimed.

Just then three men slouched in, claiming Jonas' attention. They wanted to purchase some whiskey. He produced a small brown jug from behind the counter and was in the process of counting their money when another shadow eclipsed the doorway. Looking up, he waved the newcomer over.

"Ah, Mr. Göbel," Jonas said. "Come in, come in. Got somebody you need to meet."

A jovial man entered the cramped room. Dressed neatly, he was wearing a jacket, clean corduroy slacks, and had a small bowler hat sitting squarely on his head. It was apparent he was a new wayfarer in the wilderness and not a long-time citizen.

"Sorry," Jonas said. "I didn't get you folks' name."

"O'Brien," Patrick offered his hand. "Patrick and Helen O'Brien."

"Pleased to meet you," Hans said, giving Patrick a firm handshake. "And who's this fine, strapping gentleman?"

"This is Connell," Patrick replied. "He's a little busy right now with that peppermint Mr. Napoleon gave him."

"Can't say's I blame him," Hans leaned over to be more on Connell's level. "I'm partial to peppermint myself." He winked at Connell before straightening back up. Turning to Patrick, he said, "Prefer it in schnapps though."

"From what Jonas tell us," Patrick said. "You're headed to Spadra Landing."

"That's correct. Bought us some land up that way from the speculators."

"We're headed to the Boston Mountains ourselves. We've got 180 acres there."

"We'll be neighbors then," Hans said. "We're just getting off at Spadra Landing. Our land is in the Boston's too. You should come meet the wife." Hans touched the brim of his hat with the tips of his fingers and gave a deep, bow aimed at Helen. "She'll be glad to have the company of another lady for a change."

"Lead the way," Patrick said.

Once outside, Hans stepped down from the porch and pointed in the general direction of the *M. E. Parker*.

"Been arranging passage aboard the boat," he said. "Elizabeth's back in the woods here, breaking down our camp."

"How long have you been here at this settlement, Mr. Göbel?" Helen asked.

"Hans, if you don't mind ma'am," he said. "We're going to be neighbors and all."

"In that case, Hans," she nodded and smiled, "the name's Helen, not ma'am."

"Yes ma'am," he smiled impishly at her. "To answer your question, we came up from New Orleans on another steamer. I was in an all-fired hurry. Didn't want to wait the extra time it was going take for the *M. E. Parker* to be ready to ship out. Appears I should have waited though. Boat I picked wasn't going *up* the Arkansas. She was headed on to St. Louis, was just making a stop here."

"You didn't know that beforehand?" Patrick asked.

"I just told the captain I was headed into the Arkansas Territory," Hans shook his head. "He was glad to take my money and deposit me on the edge of the Arkansas Territory. I should have been more specific."

Hans brushed absently at his pants, obviously uncomfortable about his admission. "Should have made myself better understood. Been living in a tent the last three days," he tried to change the subject, "waiting on your boat. Elizabeth's been giving me fits about it too.

She's ready for a room with solid walls again."

The small procession followed a brush choked, winding trail, to the Göbel's campsite. On the way, Helen learned that Elizabeth was a midwife. She had the title of 'granny woman' in the Old Country. In her present condition, Helen couldn't believe her luck. She looked forward to meeting her new, best friend.

The two men talked about their plans and what they intended to do in their new lives. Hans had been a vintner in the Rheinhessen region of Germany. He intended to plant grapes and become the first man to produce fine wine in the New Territory. Patrick talked of plans to build a sawmill. By the time they arrived at their destination, each man had a good feel for the other.

The Göbel's campsite was nestled on a slight knoll, under a grove of pin oaks. As they approached, they could see Elizabeth was busily packing cooking utensils and bedding.

"You picked a good campsite," Patrick said. "Don't guess it was your first."

"There wasn't much high ground around here," Hans said. "This was the best we could do."

A mosquito lit on his forearm. A quick swat and a small red smear told where the bloodsucker had been.

"Figured we'd take advantage of what little breeze there might be to keep these little buggars at bay." Turning back toward his camp, he called out, "Hey woman. Look what I brought." He threw a quick smile at Helen, "Company."

Introductions were made with Elizabeth paying the most attention to Connell. Connell, for his part, took up with Elizabeth immediately. Something he rarely did with strangers. Then everyone took to the task at hand, getting the campsite broke down. Helen pitched in, helping with the kitchen items. Patrick and Hans began folding the tent, and Connell continued to work on his peppermint stick. In no time the chore was complete, and the new friends were moving everything toward the riverbank, then onto the boat.

By dusk, all the new passengers were settled into their quarters on the *M. E. Parker*, and it was once again on the river. The Göbel's cabin was near the O'Brien's on the Hurricane Deck. The Ranklin's, Patrick learned later, was shoehorned into cramped quarters on the main deck, below the boiler deck, down among the deckhands and cargo. Benjamin's bribery had saved a few pennies, but his accommodations lacked all niceties.

Before good dark, the *M. E. Parker* passed Arkansas Post. Not seeing a flag on shore to indicate passengers wanting to be picked up, Captain Clements continued upriver. He would run the river day and night until it got too shallow. That might come above Little Rock at a place called Petit Jean. A large spine of mountain there formed a bluff on the south shore. In front of it, there was an underwater rock shelf that stretched on across the river. At low water, it formed a dam-like barrier. When there wasn't enough water, it prevented even shallow drafted steamboats from ascending further upriver. With the recent rains, that shouldn't be a problem though. Time would tell. Still, he posted lookouts forward under strict orders.

"We don't need the lead men to mark the bottom for depth," Captain Clements shouted.

"Sir?" the first mate asked.

"Keep a weather eye out for snags, Mr. Lewis."

"Aye, aye, sir."

5

Morning found Patrick leaning on the top deck railing, enjoying a blazing sunrise as the *M. E. Parker* pushed up the Arkansas River. His body draped heavily against the brass railing. His brown eyes searched for answers. Was there a pot-of-gold at the end of this rainbow? Or, like all the other endeavors he'd pursued, was this one going to be *fool's gold* too?

Fishing his meerschaum pipe from his shirt pocket, he packed the burnished bowl with Cavendish tobacco. A blend of Virginia tobacco and bourbon. The sweet of the tobacco seemed to settle his stomach after a good meal. It also settled his mind when he had to think. Maybe he'd thought too much already.

Expanding his chest, he drew the smoke deep into his lungs. The bite felt good. Exhaling slowly, thick smoke leaked from the corners of his mouth and dribbled out his nose. It lingered momentarily under the brim of his hat before being swept away in the crisp breeze.

His thoughts were a thousand miles away. The soft hiss of water flowing around the hull of the boat filled his sunburned ears. The constant throb of the steam engine married with his heartbeat. From the surface of the dingy water rose the rich, musty odor of eons of decayed leaves and moist earth. It was so strong that it filled his head and stained the air with the life it held. Maybe there was promise here.

Once more his mind retreated to County Cork, where he'd been born among its green hills. It was there he learned his trade. It was there he lost his heart to Helen O'Flanehan.

Young and poor, with little more than his name to offer, he convinced her to tie the knot. They had chosen to honor their ancestors by partaking in the ancient Celtic custom of *handfasting*. Their hands were physically tied together, signifying they were committed, tied to each other. They entered into the marriage contract for *'a year and a day'*. If Helen had decided, at the end of a year, that she no longer wanted to be married to him, she could have walked away. There would have been no mark on her name. She had stayed.

He thought back to his father's wedding day toast.

"When the roaring flames of your love have burned down to embers, may you both find that you've married your best friend!"

He could honestly say this had proven to be the case. Helen had stuck by him through one hard time after another. Every time a decision had to be made, he discussed the options with her. She offered her thoughts and they chose how they would proceed.

Such was the decision to leave County Cork. In the pubs and at firesides, Patrick had marveled at the tales of ships and sailing. Like stout ale, adventure laced every conversation. Stories of faraway lands and strange people tugged at his Irish wanderlust. He'd tried to fight it. He'd tried to settle down. But it would take a stronger will than his to deny the pull.

One evening he had approached her with the idea of America and the promise it held. She asked a few questions, he answered as best he could, and after cleaning up the supper dishes, they began packing. In a matter of weeks, they were boarding a ship for America.

Patrick thought his carpentry skills would serve him well wherever he went. He'd learned the shipbuilding trade in the shadows of Charles Fort, like his father before him. But upon arrival in New York, he could only find intermittent work. Having to watch every penny, they'd been forced to live in the crowded tenements along Pearl Street in the Five Points district. There, fighting and drinking seemed to be the main occupations of the men. Prostitution, the main occupation for many of the women.

Lost with his ghosts, the morning sun continued its sluggish ascent into the eastern sky. Patrick watched the shafts of light tiptoe across the boat's wake, slicing at the waves. The sparkle of the multicolored beams reminded him of the Irish rainbows of his youth. Maybe it was an omen. A good one at last. Lost in his thoughts, he failed to hear Hans walk up.

"Mind if I join ya?"

Hans had stopped a few feet away, not wanting to intrude upon another man's meditations. Patrick was finding a lot of things to like about this friendly German. He was open and seemed to be honest in his dealings with others. He was gracious to Helen and respectful to his own wife. And he'd taken quite the shine to young Connell. Hans was the type of man you could ride the river with, so to speak. A man you'd hope to get as a neighbor.

"There's plenty of room," Patrick said, making a broad sweep of his hand indicating the wide river, its banks choked with willows and cane thickets. "Welcome."

Making his way across the wooden deck, Hans joined Patrick at the rail. Taking out a meerschaum pipe of his own, he filled its bowl, struck a Lucifer match and applied it to the tobacco. Unlike Patrick's plain bowl, Hans' was carved with grape leaves and pheasants. He waited until smoke was pumping out, creating a small fog around his face, before he continued.

"Got a serious set to your jaw," Hans said. "Something eating at you?"

"Just plowing a field, by turning it over in my mind," Patrick laughed. Straightening, he knocked the last of the tobacco from his pipe. "Enjoying the smell of promise in this new land."

"I'll join you then if you don't mind," Hans said. "Sounds like a thing two can do as well as one."

Neither man talked for a long time, each lost in his own thoughts. They watched alligator gar roll in the murky water. White egrets filled the treetops like fresh fallen snow. The boat neared a sharp bend in the serpentine river and the captain pulled a long blast of the whistle. At the sudden clap of noise, the egrets rose in a white cloud of wings. Flying low to the water, they crossed in front of the boat to the other side of the river. From the far bank, the woman-like scream of a panther floated on the air. It was not an angry sound. The panther was just putting all God's creatures on notice. She was ending her nightly prowling. They were safe for now.

The sound of the steady thump, thump, thump of the steam piston; the constant hiss of leaking steam; and the rhythmic splash of the paddlewheel all combined with hypnotic effect. The raw beauty of the river made a man think anything was possible in this new age.

"Let's talk with the captain." Hans broke the trance. "See what information he can give us on our destination."

"Sounds good," Patrick agreed.

The pilothouse sat on top of the front portion above the Texas deck, slightly ahead of the twin smokestacks. The two men entered the spacious cabin from a side door. A crewman was standing at the large wheel, both hands firmly grasping the spoke handles. To one side, Captain Clemens sat in his plush, leather chair watching the river through the pilot house's large, glass windows. When needed, he would give the steersman instructions.

"May we impose?" Hans asked.

"Gentlemen," Captain Clemens said. "Welcome to my world. Come in, come in Mr. O'Brien. Who's your friend?"

"This is Hans Göbel." Patrick waited until the two men shook hands. "We were wondering if you could furnish us with a little information."

"I'll do what I can."

The captain adjusted himself in his chair. He wanted to look at a man when he talked to him, but he needed to keep an eye on the business at hand, too. His face relaxed as he watched the steady current roll under his boat.

"The river is waltzing nicely this morning."

"What can you tell us about our destination?" Patrick asked.

"And, where might your final destination be, gentlemen?"

"Eventually to the Boston Mountains," Patrick said. "But on the river, as far as Spadra Landing."

The captain motioned for the men to sit down. They took a seat on the couch with their backs to the rear windows. The captain kept his eyes primarily on the river, glancing periodically at his guests.

"Lots of water between here and Spadra," he said.

Rustling through neatly stacked maps, he pulled one out and placed it on top of a small table. Looking at his watch, he scribbled notes in a journal, then continued.

"But we'll cover it quicker than you'd think." A snort of a laugh added emphasis to his words. "Quicker'n they did in canoes and keelboats, and in a lot more comfort."

Patrick agreed with the quicker part but couldn't help but smile at the mention of comfort. A commodity Helen was still searching for.

The conversation soon took on the quality of a lecture as Captain Clemens extolled the benefits of steam travel, landings they would make, and history of the area. There would be a number of possible landings as they pushed up the river. They'd only pull in if the flags were flying. But they would definitely layover at Little Rock.

"Little Rock is now the capital of the Territory. A bustling place," he said. "We'll tie up there overnight. Got lots of cargo to offload. It'll give you folks a chance to see the sights."

"Hope there's more sights to see than where I boarded," Hans said with a shake of his head. "Nothing there but mosquitoes and leaches."

"Plenty of both waiting on you where you're headed." A broad smile split Clemens' face. "But most of the leaches will be the two-legged kind."

"The world must be full of them then," Patrick said. "I left plenty of them behind me too."

"There's no shortage of 'em," Hans agreed.

The captain pardoned himself for a minute and jotted down something in his journal. Probably something about his progress up the river. While he was doing that, Patrick glanced out the window and saw a large clearing on the riverbank. It had a few deserted structures on it that appeared to be man-made.

"That clearing," he said. "Don't look natural. Did people live along here?"

"Sharp eye," Clemens said. "Before my time on the river, they say there were thousands of Quapaw living here. Ain't but a few hundred of 'em now. Once we get above Little Rock things change. That's where the mountains first start. Then you'll see evidence of Cherokee."

"You mean there's Indians where we're headed?" Hans asked.

"Not so you'd notice," Clemens said. "But some." The captain told of the miles and miles of deserted towns and gardens they would see. Mostly devoid of anything but volunteer crops of corn, squash, and beans. "The three sisters, the Indians called the crops. Cause they grew together. The corn provided the stalks for the beans to grow up and the squash keep weeds down. But they's few Indians there now. The government put them off their land. Moved 'em west of Fort Smith five years ago."

"Just up and made them move?" Hans asked.

"Carried a bunch of 'em myself," the captain nodded. "Made good money at it too. Crammed as many as we could on the boat. Pulled a barge behind with as many as it would hold. A sad sight."

"The way you put it sounds cold," Patrick said. "Just taking their land and making them leave. That don't seem right."

Clemens turned in his chair to look directly at the two men. His eyebrows knitted with a look of concern and amazement. "How'd you think you were getting your land?" He waited a moment for it to sink in. "Did you think no living soul wanted it before you?"

Patrick felt like he'd been punched in the gut. He'd assumed this land was wild. Land no one had ever tamed. Land the government had purchased from France in bulk. The feeling of having made a mistake returned.

"I didn't know people were forced off this land," he said. "All I know is that we bought and paid for our parcels. Sounds like our land is stolen land." He swallowed to keep a guilty lump down.

"Most folks don't think that way," the captain said. "I guess the fact that you realize the wrong makes you a better man than most."

Captain Clemens returned his attention to the river. Taking out his pocket watch, he looked at the map and made another entry in his journal.

"Watch for shallow water at this next sand bar," he said to the steersman. "She has a habit of shifting around. Probably find the main current on the south side."

They were past the danger of the shoal and into the next deep pool before he returned his attention to his guests.

"Some folks think Indians are little more than animals, if that," he finally said. "Unable to think and do like regular folks. Let me tell you a story about the very *first* school ever built in this Territory. A little place called

Dwight Mission." Clemens pointed at a spot on the map. "You'll see it there a smidgen above Lewisburg."

The captain glanced out the window at the river, then resumed.

"There was a school there. First real school in the state. Taught students the three R's. Reading, 'riting, and 'rithmetic," he said. "Students were good too. Good as any educated dandy from back east." He ran a hand over his beard in contemplation of something. "Now, where you're going," he said. "Up in the Bostons, your neighbors ain't gonna have much book learning. Few of 'em will be able to do more than make a mark for their name." Clemens used his familiar pipe stem as a pointer for emphasis.

"But them students in that school was smart," he continued. "I know 'cause I helped move that school. Moved it west. Out in Indian Territory, cause the students were all Cherokee."

Conversation dropped off sharply as each man searched his own scales of right and wrong. Patrick knew what it felt like to be at the bottom of the barrel. Five Points had taught him that lesson well. If he ever got the chance to even things out, he would.

Hans was the first to break the silence.

"Our land isn't on the River though. We're back up in the mountains. On Little Piney Creek. Maybe there weren't any Indians up there."

"You may be away from the Arkansas." Clemens rummaged through a collection of maps. Finally finding the one he wanted, he spread it out and tapped his finger at a section where a number of inverted V's indicated mountains. "But you're smack dab in the middle of contended ground."

"What contended ground?" Patrick asked.

"These mountains are where the Osage and Cherokee rubbed shoulders," the captain said. "Lots of killing took place there. There'll probably be more."

"You mean we need to worry about Indian attacks?" Hans asked.

"It's not just Indians who kill over land squabbles," Clemens said. "That's some rough country you're heading into. Still contention over old Spanish Land Grants. You keep a sharp eye."

"What if there are still Indians there?" a worried look clouded Han's face.

"If there's any Cherokee left in them mountains," Clemens said, "serve you well to consider 'em friends and good people. Treat 'em accordingly. Just my take on it. You'll have to make your own bed."

The conversation changed to stories of Indian wars, fur traders and riverboat gamblers. Along toward mid-morning, the two friends took their leave of the captain. He needed to attend to his business, and they needed to address their own set of problems. Their next order of business was to find a quiet place to compare notes.

A borrowed map showed the mountains north of the river in good detail. Using it, and the rough maps they'd been given along with their land purchase, they began to build a picture of what lay ahead.

Hans' land was on a stream named Owens Creek. It appeared to be in a long valley. The valley drained into Devil's Fork, which in turn emptied into the Little Piney Creek, which then made its way south to the Arkansas River near the uprooted Dwight Mission School.

Patrick's parcel was in a spot further north. If he could believe the map, it appeared to be a box canyon on a drainage called Cliffy Creek. This creek emptied directly into the Little Piney a mile or so above where Devil's Fork entered the Piney. On the map, Owens Creek and Cliffy Creek looked to be fairly close, but in mountains, close is relative. A little below the two creeks entrance into the Little Piney appeared to be a community named Union Township. They would have some neighbors.

Over the next few days, the two men tried to imagine what they would find at the end of their journey. They began by looking at the shoreline and speculating. Each day seemed to bring a new perspective.

"Okay, this is the Arkansas Territory," Hans said each morning. "This is what we can expect."

But each day their view would change. What started as swamps and canebrakes changed into hardwood forests. Those changed from pin oak flats into rolling hills of hickory, then to mountains and pine trees.

Between the mouth of the Arkansas and Little Rock, other than the geography of the riverbanks, there was little to distinguish one day from another. Everything seemed to be passing by peaceably. And it was, at least as far as Patrick knew.

6

On the evening before the *M. E. Parker* arrived in the Territorial Capitol, there came a knock at the Göbel's stateroom door. Elizabeth gently swung the door outward to discover who their visitor might be. She was greeted by the smiling green eyes of her newest friend, Helen.

"Connell's asleep," Helen began. "Patrick's watching him and making his big plans." She waggled her head and with each index finger, made circular motions in the air above her head.

Elizabeth giggled and jerked her thumb over her shoulder, indicating the room behind her. "Hans' at it too."

"Care to join me in my evening constitutional?" Helen said. "I try to do a little walking each day. Figure it's good for the baby."

"I would enjoy a little fresh air," Elizabeth said. With a quick glance back into the room she called to Hans. "We girls will be back shortly."

A mumbled incoherent something was all she got in return. Elizabeth slipped a blue shawl from a hook by the door, stepped outside, and draped it over her shoulders. A gentle push closed the stateroom door with a secure thud. Turning, she joined Helen on the outer deck. Together the women headed down the port side of the ship walking slowly toward the stern.

Except for a severe thunderstorm experienced around Vicksburg, Helen had made the circuitous promenade of their deck every evening since New Orleans. Sometimes she'd made it alone, but usually, Patrick and Connell accompanied her. Now she had another woman to share it with. And that was a pleasant new experience.

The bond between the two women was growing quick and strong. Together, they strolled down the deck, arms entwined, exchanging small talk. With the sweet aroma of honeysuckle saturating the evening breeze, they shared secrets that they would never admit to their husbands. Dreams were whispered, future hopes compared. And tonight, they discussed all the possibilities for shopping with tomorrow's landing.

As they made their way around the front section of the hurricane deck, they were greeted by singing coming from below. A rhythmic beat floated up along with what sounded like people clapping in time. Helen gave Elizabeth's hand a gentle squeeze. In the fading light, she flashed a conspiratorial smile and nodded her head.

"Let's go see!" they said in unison.

Excitedly, they descended the two flights of stairs to the main deck. At the bottom, they discovered a group of passengers crowded near the front of the boat. Torch baskets, burning their oily cloth scraps, cast a flickering glow over the assemblage. Past the crowd, a circle of black deckhands, bare from the waist up, were slapping their thighs, arms and chest in a timed beat accompanied by a song. Inside the circle, two well-built black men, hopped around on one leg, dancing to the beat. As the two women drew close, they could make out the words.

> *Juba dis and Juba dat,*
> *And Juba kissed da yellow cat,*

You sift the meal and ya gimme the husk,
You bake the bread and ya gimme the crust,
You eat the meat and ya gimme the skin,
And that's the way,
My mama's troubles begin

The lively tune, along with the movements of the participants, brought a smile to Helen's freckled face. It reminded her of an Irish jig. The dancers would end their turn with a stomp and long drag of the foot, calling out *'dog scratch'*. They would then rejoin the outer circle only to be replaced by two more men who'd take center stage and repeat the song.

"That looks like so much fun," Elizabeth said.

"I wonder what it's called," Helen asked.

"They call it the Juba dance."

A couple standing nearby both answered at the same time. The simultaneous answer caused the couple to look at one another and laugh. All around passengers clapped in time with the dancers. Everyone seemed to be having a good time.

Unnoticed, the Ranklin brothers loitered in the dark inner passageway with a few other men. A brown whiskey jug made the rounds. The younger Ranklin had noticed the women's arrival, and through the dull roar of drunken confidence, a glimmer of an idea worked its way into his skull. He began to worm his way close to Helen. He approached from her left side, away from Elizabeth. The constant movement of the passengers hid his intentions until he got close to her ear.

"Them nikked darkies work you up?" he whispered.

His words reached Helen's ear about the same time his stench attacked her nose. It was a sharp, salty mix of dried sweat, stale smoke with a little livestock manure added in for body. The stench, and his words, combined for a double assault. She wheeled to face her assailant. In the flickering light from the deck torches, she found a slovenly blob of humanity hovering next to her.

"I beg your pardon!" she said.

"You heard me," he replied. A sly sneer curled the corner of his piggish mouth. His tongue snaked out and wet his upper lip. "They make you want a real man?" His heavy eyebrows jerked sharply up, then down, as if they were conspirators in some dark deed.

"How dare you!"

Before she thought and before he could react, she slapped him across his left ear with her open palm. It was a race to see which would get redder first, his boxed ear or his face.

"Why you little tramp..."

A look of surprise and anger transformed and twisted Jacob's face. Instinctively, he drew back his own hand in preparation to strike back.

The pop of Helen's hand against Jacob's face didn't carry far above the noise of the jubilant crowd, but Elizabeth heard it. She spun around to see what was wrong. Jacob's odor slammed into her nose as she turned. Her automatic reaction was to wave a hand in front of her face, in a useless attempt to dispel some of the stink.

"What's going on!" she demanded. Seeing the raised hand, she stepped between Jacob and Helen, to protect her pregnant friend.

"Weren't talking to you."

Jacob's voice trembled with anger as his right hand unclenched and moved to rub his left cheek.

Others in the crowd started turning to the sound of an altercation. Their stares registered slowly in Jacob's whiskey-soaked brain. He realized he needed to gain control of his emotions, but it wasn't happening quick enough.

"I've a good mind to tell my husband of your insolence," Helen said over Elizabeth's shoulder. "He'd teach you some manners."

The older Ranklin had trailed along with his brother. He'd slipped around and was standing behind the two women while they confronted his younger brother. He pushed up close behind Helen, nudging her back with his stomach. This caused Helen to stagger into Elizabeth. Both women turned to see who was butting into the situation now.

"I'd leave your husband out of it," Benjamin said, his tone flat and more menacing than Jacobs. "My brother wus just being friendly."

The women assessed the new threat. Something was different about this newcomer. He too stunk, but not as foul as the first. The original threat was dressed in greasy, stained canvas. The second dressed in animal furs. Still, there was something more that separated the two. Something about the bigger man was sinister and cold. His black eyes didn't shine. They were dead.

"What he said was not friendly," Helen stood her ground, color flushing her cheeks. "I'm not common trash to be talked to like that."

"Let it lie, lady."

The mountain of a man spoke in a soothing voice, but it was tinged with a warning that didn't go unnoticed by either woman.

"A simple 'not interested' is plain enough."

"My husband should teach you both a lesson."

Helen was fuming mad, but she sensed the danger. She just couldn't back down.

"Go tell your husband," Benjamin's voice chilled the night air like an ice storm. "Good way for you to become a widow. Then you might learn you need a real man."

Helen stood fuming. Words piled up in her mind, creating a verbal log jam that galled the back of her throat. She searched for the right ones, but before she could pick them out, Elizabeth grabbed her by the arm and began pulling her away. Helen's green eyes snapped fire at the two brothers as her friend forced her to back away.

"Let's get away from this filth."

Elizabeth spoke loud enough to be heard fifteen feet away. People turned, glancing nervously at the two brothers. The crowd began to pull away, creating a no-man's land around them. "I feel slimy just being near them," she said.

Elizabeth turned her back to the two Ranklin's, and started moving away from them, pulling her friend along with her. Helen glared back over her shoulder, fire sparking in her eyes.

Unimpressed by the reaction of the crowd, the brothers watched them retreat. The younger one smiled and wiped his mouth with the back of his hand. The older brother just stared unconcerned with those black eyes.

Elizabeth continued to move Helen away. Herding her toward the stairs and to the upper deck, she forced her up and away from the danger. As the threat began to fade, Helen started shaking uncontrollably.

"I'm so mad," she said. "I don't know what to do."

"Just ignore them," Elizabeth said. "If you did away with all the low life's in this country, there'd only be six people left to talk to."

"Six?" Helen asked.

"Yes," Elizabeth said with a smile. "Me and you, Patrick and Hans, Connell and Jesus."

Helen couldn't help but laugh, which quickly turned into a giggle. As much a release from the tension of the moment as it was from the humor of Elizabeth's statement. Smiling, the two women continued up the stairs to their deck.

"I'd best make another turn around the deck," Helen said. "I'm too upset to go to my stateroom now. I don't know if I should tell Patrick or not. And I know he'd see it on my face if I went inside now."

"Don't bother him with such trash," Elizabeth said. "We'll just keep our distance from those two. Pretty soon we'll be off the boat, and we'll never have to see either of them again."

"I guess you're right," Helen said. "No need to borrow trouble."

Arm in arm, the women made a couple more circuits around the deck. By the time they returned to their staterooms, they had their emotions under control.

Back downstairs, the Ranklin's were having their own conversation.

"Uppity bitch," Jacob growled his face contorted in a mask of hate. "She'll regret the way she treated me."

"You might'a asked for some of that."

Jacob cast a quick glance at the stairway going to the upper decks. "What'll we do if she does tell her husband?" A look of concern had replaced the hate on Jacob's face. The possibility of a mad husband on the prod for his hide started to soak through his liquor-soaked brain. "What if he comes looking for us?"

"Ain't no need for concern," the older brother said. "If'n he shows, we'll take care of it." Benjamin ran his grimy fingers through his thick black beard, looked up at the moonless night and spit in the general direction of the river. It splattered on the worn, wooden deck; ten feet short of the railing. "We got bigger fish to fry."

"Bigger fish," Jacob said. "Like what?"

"Like who stole Cliffy Hollow out from under us," Benjamin's eyes narrowed.

"You said our two sections on Devil's Fork is good land." Jacob was having trouble moving on to a different subject. "We got good sections, didn't we?"

"We did. They're good sections. But Cliffy Hollow, that's the best piece of ground in the whole drainage. I intend to get it back."

"What you plan to do?" Jacob asked. "That is, once we find out who's got it."

"We'll convince him to sell it."

Benjamin looked hard into his brother's face. "Or he'll wish he had."

Everything looked fresh the next morning as the *M. E. Parker* shouldered its way into the south shore of the Arkansas River at Little Rock. It found a berth between the steamboats *Allegheny* and the *Catawba*. A smattering of smaller paddle wheelers, flatboats, and rafts littered the bank for a couple of hundred yards in each direction. A handful of canoes and rowboats plied the smooth, slow running current that snuck past the territorial capitol. But above the sounds of the boilers of the boats; above the noise of loading and unloading material and the shuffling of boatmen going about their jobs; above it all, you could hear the city.

An ever-present hum of people, wagons, horses, and dogs floated down the steep bank. The sounds of a city hung in the upper reaches of the air and couldn't be disguised, not even by the pleasant, morning breeze.

Looking across the river to the flatter north shore, Patrick could see quite a few buildings. They appeared older and worn. That was where the Southwest Trail first deposited its travelers when they met the obstacle of the river. They would have hung up there temporarily, before making it across to continue their southern migration. But the newest construction was on the southern banks, above the flood plain. Little Rock was a going concern.

"I like what I see," he said.

"It's not Mouth of Arkansas," Hans agreed. "That's for sure."

Patrick couldn't help but notice the geological change from the swampy, lowlands where they'd entered the Territory. But what was striking was the change in the attitude of the people. Little Rock was open and friendly. Frontiersmen and businessmen alike populated the walkways or crisscrossed the dusty streets. Churches were everywhere. People seemed to have a purpose. They spoke greetings to one another as they went about their business. If this was what lay ahead of them in their new home, then his decision might not have been a mistake.

As soon as breakfast was out of the way, the two women took Connell and left the boat for a shopping trip. Helen wanted to buy some material for clothes. She needed thread, buttons, woolen cloth, as well as linen, and she needed suspenders for Patrick.

Elizabeth needed to check on some medical supplies. She was running low on opium for pain; calomel for purging the body; and cinchona for treating malaria. These would probably not be readily available in Spadra and impossible to obtain where they were going. Captain Clemens gave them directions to two new establishments that should suit their needs.

Not wanting to spend the day shopping for calico or medicine, Patrick and Hans walked up the steep bank and into town. They wanted to explore. They found lots of new construction, including the start for a new courthouse for the Territory. By noon, they figured they'd seen enough and decided to get something to eat.

"Let's find a tavern," Hans suggested. "I need something wet. And I want to check out the talent of the local brewers."

Patrick gave in quickly to the idea. Everything had been looking up and maybe it was time he rethought his penance. "I could use a wee dram myself."

Their search was soon rewarded by a sprawling structure, the Hinderliter House, a few blocks from the riverbank. The jovial buzz escaping from inside indicated a well-used and popular establishment. Once inside, it took a moment for their eyes to adjust to the dark interior.

Bear oil lamps were placed strategically around the room to give off some light. The bar itself was nothing fancy, but utilitarian in design, made of mahogany or some other dark wood. It was waist high and stretched twelve feet down one side of the room. Behind it, a large mirror reflected the activity of the patrons. Scattered along its length were shelves with various bottles and jugs. On the opposite wall was a large painting of a voluptuous, naked woman reclining on a couch under a tree.

The rest of the room was filled with tables, most of which were occupied. Making their way through a haze of smoke, Patrick and Hans headed for the bar.

"What'll it be, gents?" the bartender chirped.

"I'd like a beer," Hans said.

"Make mine a whiskey," Patrick quickly added.

"If the blamed Temperance Society has their way," the bartender said, "beer's all I'll be able to serve."

"Place is getting too civilized," a patron chimed in.

"Don't fret yer'self 'bout them durn Methodist," a muleskinner sitting nearby offered. "They talk big, but it's just for show. I allow as how I saw that preacher himself, out behind the livery, pulling on a jug."

This brought a round of thunderous laughter from those standing nearby. Someone slapped the muleskinner on the back and dust puffed out of his coat. That was followed by another round of laughter. Then the talk moved on to another subject.

Patrick and Hans enjoyed the exchange with a smile and the nod of their heads. They paid for their drinks and moved to an open table near the front door. From here they could have some privacy in their conversation and still watch the comings and goings on the broad street outside. Patrick proposed a toast to his new friend.

"May God hold us in the hollow of his hand," he said.

Hans raised his beer mug to the toast then brought the foamy brew to his lips. Patrick threw his first whiskey into the back of his throat. The burn felt good after a long dry spell. A plump barmaid approached. As she passed a nearby table, a man in hunting garb slapped her on the rump. He said something Patrick didn't quite catch but judging from her reaction she must have liked it. She grinned back at the man, exposing eight or nine brown stained teeth.

"You fella's hungry?" she aimed her question to Hans. "We got beef dodgers and pepperpot."

From Han's puzzled expression, Patrick knew he didn't know what she was offering. He probably knew that cornmeal and minced beef was called dodgers, but pepperpot was a dish the German probably hadn't been exposed to. Very popular back in New England, it was simple and filling fare when prepared properly.

"A sort of stew," Patrick said. "Tripe and doughballs."

Hans made a sour face. "Just the dodgers if you please."

"Pepperpot for me," Patrick smiled, "and another whiskey."

As she walked away, Patrick noticed two men sitting near the back wall. They seemed to be taking a serious interest in Hans and himself. At first, it gave him a sense of unease, but he soon passed it off as his imagination, since he didn't recognize either man.

Hans brought Patrick's attention back to their ongoing conversation, by observing their journey was nearing an end. In just a few days they would be leaving the river and headed north to their homesteads.

"Won't be long now," Hans said. "You know we'll have to start from scratch."

"Lots of work ahead for sure," Patrick replied absently.

The hair on the back of Patrick's neck began to tingle again. Something about the two men just wasn't right. He didn't know anyone here in Little Rock. Or in the whole of the Arkansas Territory for that matter. But the two men did seem familiar. He stole another look toward the back of the room. Both men were watching them, of that there was no doubt.

"See those two men?" he asked Hans. "At the back table."

Hans sat his half-empty beer down and turned in his chair. At first, he didn't see who Patrick might mean. When the two men stood and started walking in their direction, Hans asked, "The two coming this way?"

"You know them?"

"Think their name's Ranklin, or something like that," Hans replied. "They were at Mouth of Arkansas."

The two brothers made their way slowly toward the front table. Due to the dimness of the room and the thick facial hair, Patrick couldn't make out their expressions. But their destination was clear. Drawing nearer, he could see their hollow eyes and his hand automatically searched for the handle of his knife.

"You got a problem with us?" the younger and dirtier of the two demanded.

"Why would I have a problem with you?" Patrick asked. "We've never met."

"Ain't nobody mentioned our names?" the young one snarled.

"If they have," Patrick shot back. "I don't remember hearing it." His ears flushed red. These two were spoiling for a fight, but he didn't know why. In another time and place, he might have obliged them. But he'd only had the one drink, so he wasn't about to lose his head and just start swinging. Maybe these two had already had too much to drink and were mistaking him for somebody else.

The younger of the two had been doing all the talking up to this point. While he ran his mouth, he shifted from one foot to the other. The older one was quiet and kept his feet planted firmly in one place. This was the one to watch. If real trouble started, it would come from him.

"Name's Ranklin," the older one finally said. "Benjamin Ranklin. This here's my brother Jacob. We're on the *M. E. Parker,* same as you."

Realization came slowly to Patrick. This was the other family Mr. Jonas had warned him about back at the trading post. He'd promised he would hold his opinion until he met them himself. So far, he'd have to agree with

Mr. Jonas' assessment. No one who met them would consider these two ruffians the salt of the earth.

"Come to think of it, I have heard the name." Patrick motioned to Hans and himself.

"I understand you're headed to Spadra Landing same as us. Maybe we're going to be neighbors."

Something in the attitude of the older Ranklin seemed to ease. The tight lines around his eyes relaxed. For some reason, he'd been expecting trouble. Now that it wasn't coming, the chip on his shoulder was not quite so big. The younger of the two remained just as surly as he had been.

"Doubt if we'll be neighbors," he sneered. "Full-grown men live where we're going."

"Where might that be?"

Hans made a valiant attempt to join the conversation that had so far been directed at Patrick alone.

"The roughest mountains between heaven and hell," the fatter of the two replied, puffing his chest out like a strutting tom turkey.

"Don't even have the decency to run North and South like respectable mountains. They run crosswise, East and West."

"The Boston's!" Hans said. "I noticed that from the maps and thought it strange." He let the jibe about his suspected manhood drop unanswered.

"That's exactly where we *are* going!" Patrick wasn't going to let the challenge drop. "I consider myself full grown."

"Don't get worked up," the older Ranklin cooed. "My brother's just going on stories I've told him. But the Little Piney valley can be a mean place for a tenderfoot."

"Yeah," Jacob butted in. "The Little Piney valley is wild and mean. Maybe there's a tamer part of the Ozarks where you're headed."

"We're headed for the Little Piney too," Hans replied. "I'm headed to a place called Owen's Creek. Maybe you know it."

"I know every inch of that valley," Benjamin said.

"Our place is on Devil's Fork," Jacob curled his upper lip in disgust. "You'll have to cross our land to get to yours." He turned toward his older brother for confirmation.

Patrick noticed that the younger Ranklin was still biting off his words. He was still spoiling for a fight. It was obvious he was a bully, trying to get his bluff in on an opponent. He was trying to use the boom of his voice and his constant strutting to look bigger than he was. Maybe he impressed himself with the sound of his own voice. Of the two, this one would dry gulch you. He'd strike from ambush with no compunction. But if he had to face a man on equal terms, he'd back down.

But the calmer disposition of the older brother spoke volumes. His size, the way he carried himself and his self-confidence said he was in charge of the two. A bear of a man, he would dry gulch you or come at you head-on. It was obvious he'd been tested and hadn't come up short too many times. The lack of expression on his hard face exposed the steel that lay beneath.

Patrick felt a small twinge of guilt for what he was thinking. He was glad Hans would have to put up with these neighbors and not him. They were going to be a handful to whoever shared their boundary line.

"My brother discovered that valley," the younger, fatter of the two said. "First white man to lay eyes on it. Ain't that right Benjamin?"

"That's right," the older man said.

"Found it when I was trading with the Indians. Later, I run across a man down at Arkansas Post who had a Spanish Land Grant to the whole thing. So, I bought it from him lock-stock-and-barrel. Cost me a whole winter's worth of furs."

"If you own it," Patrick said, "How come we have claims to parts of it?"

"The damn guv-mint." Jacob threw his hands up in the air before Benjamin could respond. "They took it. And sold it to Johnny-come-lately's like you. And we ain't about to stand for it."

The older Ranklin put his hand up to slow his brother down. "It ain't these men's fault. Not all of it leastwise. They didn't know it already belonged to someone else."

A red glow began to come back to Patrick's ears. He was making an effort to control his temper, but these two were making it hard. It was a good thing he'd only had the one drink of whiskey.

"After the Louisiana Purchase deal," the older man said, "The U.S. Courts disallowed most of the Spanish claims. I lost the entire valley, except for the two sections on Devil's Fork."

"Then I don't see how you own the whole valley," Patrick said. "The government said you didn't. They offered it for sale, and I bought my piece of it."

"After I bought it fair and square and it was stolen from me," Benjamin said in a level, cold tone. "Ain't no two ways to that. Dang politicians seen a way to steal so

68

they'd get money out of what weren't theirs." His voice grew even colder. "One day, I'll get my justice. I'll get it all back."

Hans appeared to be looking for a way to get back into the conversation and maybe cool down some of the tension in the process.

"Hey, if you know that valley so well, maybe you can tell us about the parcel Patrick bought."

Hans smiled at his two neighbors. "It's on Cliffy Creek."

"Cliffy Hollow!"

Benjamin bellowed like a prodded bull, his eyes narrowing. He spun to confront Patrick squarely. A death-shroud cold enveloped the room. "You're the bastard that stole Cliffy Hollow?"

Damning voices caused chairs around the room to scrape hard on the wooden floor. All conversation stopped. Bar patrons spun to see what the ruckus was all about. Hands moved to knives and pistols just in case the fight got bigger than the one table. Little Rock might be headed toward civilized society and statehood, but its citizens still understood violence. It there was going to be trouble they wanted to be facing it when it came.

"Watch who you call a thief."

Patrick's face flushed and his eyes went to slits. Bounding to his feet in a half-crouch, the chair he'd been sitting in tumbled behind him. The fourteen-inch knife sprang into his hand as if it had grown there. It was pointing at Benjamin's belly.

"Some full-grown men won't take that," he said.

White spittle formed in the corners of the older Ranklin's mouth. On the verge of rushing Patrick, he saw the knife in time. Patrick saw the change come to his face. The older brother knew he was facing a man who knew how to handle a blade. Patrick held the knife low, ready to strike and Ranklin's hands were empty. But his head wasn't.

"The hollow's not yours," he said. He lowered his voice to a conversational tone, his eyes still on fire, but butter wouldn't melt in his mouth.

"But I'll be fair," he continued. "I'll buy my own land back. Just so there won't be no hard feelings. I'll give you ten cents for every dollar you paid."

"Don't sound like much of a deal to me," Patrick returned the deadly stare.

"It's the only deal you'll get, Irish."

"Then I'll pass if it's all the same to you." Patrick remained crouched in a knife-fighters' stance. "I intend to raise my family on that land."

"You'll bury 'em on it."

Benjamin wheeled and stormed away, followed closely by his younger brother. When they reached the door, he stopped and looked back. No one doubted his final words. "You've been warned, Irish!"

After the Ranklin's hasty departure, it didn't take long for the tavern to return to normal. This was not the first argument the establishment had seen, and it wasn't even close to the deadliest.

Hans sat back down and sipped at his beer. "I believe you've picked up an enemy there."

Patrick raised his glass as in a toast. "May the Devil cut off the toes of our foes, that we may know them by their limping." He smiled, but his eyes didn't join in.

They ordered another round and tried to figure out what had just happened. Not being able to make much sense out of it, it was put in the back of their minds. They eventually made their way back to the *M. E. Parker.*

"No need to mention this to the womenfolk," Patrick said. "It's just a misunderstanding and in time it'll work itself out."

Hans agreed.

8

It was eight o'clock the next morning before the *M. E. Parker* could back away from the landing. Captain Clemens had waited until the fog burned off for safety's sake. He was in a hurry, but there was no sense crashing into another steamboat if it could be avoided. That would slow things up even more.

Backing away from the shore, Patrick watched the side paddles churn mud from the bottom of the river, turning the water as cloudy as his thoughts. He was nearing his destination, the end of his rainbow, and he'd already made a good friend. Hans and Elizabeth were going to be the neighbors he could depend upon. But he had made enemies too. Judging from the incident in the tavern, they would be a serious threat, and he wasn't sure why.

Knocking the ashes out of his pipe, he straightened up and with a furrowed brow looked upriver. Moving away from the congestion of boats, garbage, and the stench of the city landing seemed to help his disposition. No use crying over spilled milk. This was the final leg of the river journey, and needs were afoot. He'd make his way down to the main deck and check his equipment, just to ensure it was still lashed and stowed properly.

The lower deck was where the Ranklin's were quartered, or so he'd been told. Hopefully, he wouldn't run into them today. If he did, so be it.

After checking on his equipment, he'd check in with Hans, to see how his preparations were coming. His morning planned out, he squared his shoulders and headed downstairs.

The only people stirring on the main deck were the deckhands going about their chores. A few male passengers were draped atop the cargo in various positions of collapse, sleeping off a drunk from their night ashore. The Ranklin's were not among their numbers as far as he could tell. But then, he didn't go looking for them.

Finding his equipment, he soon discovered he couldn't get to it. Among the first families to come aboard in New Orleans, his equipment was covered up by more recent boarders. From what he could see, everything was fine. The only problem with being the first loaded meant that he would be the last unloaded. With a shrug, he headed topside.

Stopping by his own stateroom he found Connell asleep and Helen working on her list of things they'd need.

"How many times are you going to write that list?" he teased.

"Patrick O'Brien," she began. "Now ain't you the one to be schooling me about lists. Just 'cause I keep mine on paper, unlike someone I know, don't mean you ain't got one in your head you been worrying to death."

Patrick laughed. There was little he could get over on his beautiful wife and that was part of her charm. She was his equal in some things, and if truth be told, she was his better in most. If they forgot something it wouldn't be in the household items. She was a stickler for detail where he was more apt to let something slip by.

"What's the name of the place where we're getting off?"

"Spadra Landing."

"Is there any town between there and our new place?" she asked.

"Nothing of any size."

"Then you'd better tend to your own list," her eyes sparkled with the challenge. "Won't be no mercantile around the corner you can run down to like in New York."

"I see I'm not gonna win this discussion," he smiled back at the love of his life. "Guess I'd best be about my business."

"Good decision," Helen agreed. "Why don't you go bother Hans. He probably needs your help."

Over the next few days, the men lost track of time with their plans to tame the wilderness. Lists were made, checked, changed, and made again. Time was spent pouring over the crude maps of the Ozark Mountains.

It was a strange land that some called mystical. It started on the northern edge of the Arkansas River Valley, and the mountains jumbled their way up into Missouri. Inside these mystic folds of earth lay their new homes and their destiny.

Between Little Rock and Spadra there were only a few landings and even fewer stops. The *M. E. Parker* churned its way west past the landmark of Galla Rock, a two-mile-long, shale bluff, forty feet high on the north bank of the river. Deserted now, the village had been the home to the Cherokee leader John Jolly. At Lewisburg, the *M. E.*

Parker stopped long enough to unload supplies and take on more wood. Moving upriver, past Dwight and Scotia, it was early afternoon when they docked at Spadra Landing. The jumping-off point for the O'Brien's, Göbel's, and the Ranklin's.

The loading and unloading of the *M. E. Parker* went like clockwork. Every hand knew what to do with little instruction. They went about their numerous tasks with a steady rhythm and a song. It had a melody that was both comforting and troubling. Comforting in its full, rich melody; disturbing in its lonesome soul.

"Have you seen the Ranklin's this morning?" Hans asked.

Patrick looked up and down the sandy riverbank. With all the comings and goings of people and supplies, he'd lost track of their new neighbors. He didn't figure it was a good habit to get into when it came to the Ranklins.

"Appears they made arrangements ahead of time," Hans said.

"They had wagons and teams waiting. Offloaded directly into them and headed off through town. Probably already on their way to Little Piney."

"We'll be a day or two behind them," Patrick said. "But we'll get there just the same."

Before dark, the *M. E. Parker* was pulling back out into the center of the river. Further up, closer to Fort Smith and Fort Gibson, the boat would have to tie up at night due to shallow water and debris. But in this section of the Arkansas, it was still wide and deep enough for the captain to navigate at night.

With a long, loud bellow on the whistle, the captain turned the bow of the boat upstream. Patrick and Hans waved goodbye to Captain Clemens who was standing outside the pilothouse. The boat was soon out of sight around the next bend.

"I guess we'd better head for the livery," Patrick said. "See what kind of livestock we can purchase."

"We'll need a couple of sturdy wagons too," Hans added.

They checked with their wives to ensure they would be all right. Then the two men, with Connell in tow, struck out down the dusty street for the edge of town and the livery stable. The smithy sold them part of what they needed and told them where they could obtain pigs, laying hens, a couple of roosters, and a few guineas.

From the smithy, each man purchased a wagon, milk cow, and a quarter horse. Hans got a team of mules to pull his heavily laden wagon into the rugged mountains. Patrick wanted a team of oxen.

He knew mules would be easier to handle, quicker, and would be better suited for planting a garden. But he needed oxen for the timber business. The oxen could handle heavier loads for longer periods. Endurance would fit his needs better than speed.

Arrangements were also made for his saws and other mill equipment to be moved to the wagon yard and stored until he was ready for them. When the time came, he would have teamsters deliver them to his mill site. Hopefully, that would be soon.

"Think they'll be all right here?" Hans asked. "Sitting out like this they might rust up."

"They'll be all right," Patrick said. "I'll cover everything with a thick coat of grease and cover them with canvas."

The next day was spent buying dry goods and packing the wagons for the trip. They bought flour, salt, sugar, coffee, bacon, and beans. Patrick stowed his tools of the trade; axes, saws, splitting malls, wedges, sharpening tools, and numerous other hand tools of the carpentry business. Hans carefully and lovingly packed his Muskateller grape stock. He was single-minded in his intention of planting a vineyard in his new homeland and starting his own tradition. Naturally, Patrick offered him plenty of encouragement in this endeavor. Then they headed up Spadra Creek, towards the mountains—toward home.

Being unfamiliar with the country, it took them two days to get across the valley floor. At the foot of Ozone Mountain, they began their climb. Another two days were devoured just getting to the top. The trip up the mountain consisted of traversing one steep switchback after another, slowly working their way higher and higher. On each semi-level bench, they would stop and rest the teams. The grade was steep and the load heavy. When they broke out on top, they gave the exhausted animals a full day to rest before heading across the top of the mountain.

"Sure is beautiful here," Helen said to Elizabeth.

"Feels like we're next to heaven, don't it?" Elizabeth agreed. "It's so quiet and peaceful."

"Not much chance of getting lost," Hans said. "Good deep wagon ruts to follow through these scrub oaks."

"Yep," Patrick said. "We're not the first to pass this way. Just hope our new neighbors aren't all like the Ranklins."

"I don't see how they could be," Elizabeth said.

"Deer," Connell said.

All eyes looked first at Connell, who was sitting on the wagon seat. They looked in the direction he was pointing. A cow elk stood in the middle of the wagon ruts, her reddish-brown face pointed directly at them. A yearling bounded out of the brush and bumped into its mother's rump before it could get stopped. Like all mothers, the cow gave it what could be called a warning look and then moved on off across the trail. The yearling looked at her, then looked around, seemed to shrug, then bounded after mom. Both were quickly swallowed up in the trees.

Connell clapped his chubby hands in glee. The four adults laughed. Things were going well. There was plenty of grass for the livestock, natural holes of water and loads of wildlife to entertain Connell. Numerous coveys of quail flushed close to the trail, sometimes startling the quarter horses. At close quarters, the sudden explosion of wings gave the humans a start too.

There were acres of timber with frequent small clearings. Many of the clearings held flocks of twenty or more turkeys chasing grasshoppers through the new grass. In one large clearing, they found a bull buffalo grazing contentedly. He raised his head and watched their small caravan pass with little concern.

They moved across the plateau and on through the small community of Hickory Flat. At Hickory Flat they found a home that doubled as a small trading post. They stopped for a while and were told to pay attention just a mile down the trail. The trail split, one fork turned off to Gillian Settlement, the other would lead them down toward Union. There was another twisting switchback that could take them down into Liddy Creek and then to Cliffy Creek, but it would be nearly impossible with the wagons. It was steep and narrow, one fit only for hogs to traverse.

"That's Piggy Steep," the man said. "On past, is the easier grade down into Union. That's where you need to go."

Taking his advice, from the fork it took another day to get down the mountain and into the Little Piney valley.

Even though they were anxious to see their new land, they thought it best to spend a day camped on the grassy banks of the Little Piney near Union, the center of their new world. In Union, they met other settlers who told them which landmarks to watch for as they moved upstream to their own land. They were assured they had purchased good land. That night at the campfire, with the smell of beans tickling their noses, the two men found it hard to ignore their excitement.

"We're at the end of the rainbow," Hans said.

"Now we'll each find our pot of gold," Patrick replied.

At first light, they were up, anxious for the last leg of their journey. The women prepared breakfast of thick-sliced bacon, eggs, coffee, and flatbread. The men hooked up harnesses and checked equipment. Before the sun had warmed the upper branches of the huge oaks, they'd hitched their teams, and together, headed up the boulder-strewn Little Piney.

At the junction of Devil's Fork, they split up. The Göbel's headed for their land on Owens Creek and the O'Brien's moved on up Little Piney to their land in Cliffy Hollow. The two families had already made arrangements to assist each other later, so the morning's goodbyes were short.

"See you in a week, yah?" Hans called over his shoulder as his wagon bounced over rocks, gravel, and driftwood.

"Helen, you take care," Elizabeth added. "Don't you be worrying none. I'll be checking on you."

Each family planned to set up camp on their own property. They would spend a few days marking and laying out their boundaries and figuring where they wanted their homes built. Then they would get together and help each other put up a house and barn. Theirs wouldn't be the log cabin affairs of most. They would build solid homes of milled lumber. Patrick would see to that, but the barns would have to come first.

With Connell already underfoot and another child on the way, the O'Brien's would get the first house. As quickly as that was accomplished, the men would start on the Göbel dwelling.

"Before I do anything else," Hans had said, "I want to get my grape stock in the ground."

"The first thing I want to do," Patrick replied, "is to walk my land. I want to find the perfect spot for the sawmill."

When the O'Brien's did see their hollow, they couldn't believe their luck. Cliffy Creek bubbled cheerfully down from the mountains in a series of clear, deep pools, punctuated with small waterfalls. It wound through the hollow, embracing stands of chinquapin, chestnut, hickory, oak, and sumac. The ridges were thick with pines and cedars. Persimmon and black walnut resided in natural clearings. Sarvis berry, dogwood, huckleberry, and blackberry bushes were everywhere. He understood why Benjamin Ranklin wanted this hollow.

So far, he hadn't seen either of the Ranklin brothers, but that was just a matter of time. The Little Piney Valley wasn't that big.

People in Union Township said the Ranklin's were building shelters up on Devil's Fork. Sooner or later, he would be rubbing shoulders with them. But for now, they would be Hans' problem. Until then, he had work to do. Find a site for the mill, decide on a homesite and break ground for a garden. Then would come the barns and before the first snow flew, he must have both families in the dry. Plenty enough to keep his mind off Ranklin's.

9

It was a week later when the Ranklin's made their presence known.

"What'cha up to, Irish?"

Surprised, Patrick wheeled around to see both Ranklin brothers materializing out of a plum thicket. Each cradled a musket in the crook of his arm. The younger brother had a silly grin on his filthy face, apparently pleased they had caught him unaware.

Patrick was sitting on a large rock, his back to the plum thicket, when the two spoke. He had just lowered a jug of water from his mouth, mentally lost in laying out the form his new cabin would take. He hadn't heard the older brother's moccasins or the heavier tread of the younger one's brogans.

"Caught me by surprise," he admitted. "Guess I'd better start paying closer attention to what's going on around me."

"Good advice," Ben took in the meadow and the surrounding hillside.

"Where's you woman and whelp?"

"Got camp set up down by the creek," Patrick nodded in that general direction. "Figuring on building a house up here on this knoll. Just mulling things over. What you think?"

The mountain man glared at Patrick, his hooded eyes cold and still. Patrick knew he was needling Benjamin by asking his opinion, but it felt good to do so.

"If we'us Injuns," Jacob smirked, "We could of had yore hair."

The two brothers made him uneasy. With his rifle leaning against a limestone rock ten feet away, he was at a definite disadvantage. All he had was the water jug and his knife.

"Well," he said. "It's a good thing there ain't Indians around anymore. I think I like the idea of keeping my scalp."

"Oh, they's Indians still around," the younger brother said.

"We cut signs of one t'other end of the hollow this very morning."

"Anyway," Benjamin's icy voice carried heavy on the dead air between them. "Indians didn't start scalping. White men did that."

"You saying I need to start worrying about white men?" Patrick asked.

"You'd best start worrying about a lot of things."

The older Ranklin's choice of words left little to the imagination. He was making a threat. A thinly veiled one at that.

Patrick's ears turned a crimson red, much like a rooster's comb when it was ready to fight. He had taken just about all the intimidation he would take from the Ranklins.

"You just dropping by for a friendly visit," he asked, "Or is there something particular on your mind?"

"We don't have friendly visits with thieves or drunks," Jacob said.

"Don't sugar coat it on my account," Patrick stood to face the two. "You got something to say to me, come right out and say it."

"You're on my land, Irish," Benjamin said.

"Seems to me we've already had this conversation," Patrick said as he walked boldly over to his rifle. Bending at the waist, he set the water jug next to the boulder. When he straightened back up, he had the rifle in his hand.

"Unless'en you want to leave that fiery young wife of yourn a widow," Jacob said, "you'd best be getting off our land."

"I've had my fill of threats." Patrick shifted the rifle in his hands.

"Either do your worst or pull foot and leave."

Patrick eased the muzzle of the rifle toward the two brothers. It was pointed at their feet, but just raising it a few inches would bring it to bare. His intentions were obvious.

Jacob shifted his feet, preparing to swing his musket into action. Before he completed the movement, Benjamin reached out his left hand and stopped his brother.

"Irish," he said. "I've warned you before. Either sell me this land or clear out. The choice is yours. Don't know how many times I have to repeat myself."

Patrick's voice too took on a crisp edge. "We've already had this conversation. I ain't selling. And I damn sure ain't leaving my land."

"One way or the other," Benjamin said, "I'm getting my land back."

Benjamin looked around as if checking to see if there were any witnesses. He focused his attention back on Patrick and continued. "The only O'Brien's who are going to remain on this land," his black eyes flashed, "are those who'll be buried here."

"Threats are cheap." Patrick locked eyes with Benjamin; the timber in his voice enforced his resolve.

"Anyone trying to force me off my land had best be prepared to find his own gravesite."

"Have it your way, Irish."

Without another word, Benjamin Ranklin turned and melted back into the plum thicket. Not even the rustle of a leaf exposed his departure. Patrick knew it was only a temporary retreat.

With a frown, Jacob wheeled and followed his brother. His departure was not as silent. If not for the racket he was making, Patrick could easily have thought it all a bad dream.

Were the brothers really threatening his life? Yes, they were. Jacob was a bully and a braggart, but Benjamin was not one to be taken lightly. He was more than capable of following through on his threats. If Patrick wouldn't sell him the land, he would look for a way to take it.

"Guess I'd better keep a weather eye out," Patrick said to the wind.

As if in answer to his words, a slight breeze moved through the trees and the leaves rattled a scratchy 'yes'.

He scanned the surrounding hardwoods. An attack could come from anywhere at any time. He'd need to keep an eye out constantly and his rifle near at hand.

10

Over the summer, the O'Brien's settled in at Cliffy Hollow. Patrick set up a pit sawmill first. It was a simple concept used since ancient times. But, instead of digging a pit, where one man worked a saw from on top and another man worked in a hole, he built his on a hillside.

The natural slope of the land allowed him to stabilize one end of the platform on the ground while the other end perched high on two rocks. This kept the log fairly level while it was being sawed into planks. It did nothing to change the fact that the man below still got covered with sawdust.

He made one more improvement. Instead of requiring two men, Patrick built a system where the saw was suspended from a pivot point on top and he could work the lumber from below all by himself. With this system, he cut the first rough lumber to be used in building his barn. Later, when he had time, he would damn up the creek and build a proper sawmill powered by a water wheel. For now, this would have to do.

When the time came to build the barn, his neighbors proved true to their word and helped with the *barn raising*. Families arrived from every end of the valley. Two families were noted, not by their presence, but by their absence.

"Where are the Ranklin's?" Hans asked.

"Maybe they're off hunting."

Patrick didn't want anything to dampen the friendly mood.

"No such thing," Hans said. "And you know it."

"You never know what people are thinking," Patrick said.

"Other than being downright lazy, they're not going to help you grow roots in this hollow."

Without help from the Ranklin's, the barn raising was a glorious affair. Children played in the clearing and the nearby woods. Women prepared food and the men worked. In a matter of one short day, a barn stood where before there had only been rough ground.

Once his barn was up, Patrick sawed enough rough lumber for the Göbel's barn. That done, he started on the waterwheel and dam. With it completed he could mill better-finished lumber that would be turned into a fine home for Helen and his children.

Patrick envisioned something special for his wife's home. Not the typical log cabin with a dirt floor that most settlers lived in. Helen's home would be grand. He drove stakes in the ground to lay out the outline on the ground, signifying the arrangement of the rooms. After the tenements of New York, this would be a palace.

"It seems awful big," Helen said as she wandered through the garden of stakes.

"We'll fill it up with kids," Patrick teased, rubbing her ever-expanding belly, "then you'll claim I didn't build it big enough."

"Where's my kitchen?"

"Over here," Patrick walked her to one corner, "toward the barn."

Standing behind her, he pulled her into a warm embrace, snuggling her back into his chest. Taking a deep inhale of her neck, he smiled and continued. "Just imagine. It will be built with milled planks, not logs. Lumber from our own mill."

"Tell me all about it." Helen sighed as she encouraged him to expand his dreams.

In the dwindling light of the late summer evening, Patrick explained just how wonderful her new home would be. Taking Helen by the hand, he walked her from stake to stake, through the make-believe rooms.

"There will be two large rooms downstairs..."

"Downstairs, you say?"

"Yes, downstairs!" Patrick faked a look of shock. "Do you think I'd let you live on the flat like simple folks?"

"You've been kissing the Blarney Stone is what I think Patrick O'Brierne." Helen used his name as it was pronounced in Ireland.

"You're talking out of your head."

"Out of me head, you say?"

Patrick grabbed playfully at his chest with both hands. "Tis a mortal wound you've delivered with your cruelty woman."

"Stop acting the fool," Helen slapped playfully at him. "Go on. Tell me about my house."

"The two main rooms will be separated by an open hallway six foot wide. Open to the front and back of the house."

"Where's my kitchen?"

"Over here," he said. "On the west side, will be the kitchen. It will be sixteen feet long and eighteen feet wide."

"That's awful big for a kitchen."

"Not at all!" Patrick winked. "I'll build you a fine big table for all our children to gather around at breakfast and supper. And I'll build places for you to keep your pots—and there'll be an indoor washbasin."

Patrick walked her across the expanse between stakes as he unfolded his plans. The excitement in his voice was contagious.

"Over here, on the east side, will be another room the same size as the kitchen. We can sit here on cold winter nights. Our children will play around our feet while I read them stories from the Bible. You'll be sitting here in your rocking chair, mending my socks."

"Have you been into Hans' special brew again," a smile born of love curled Helen's mouth.

"Your green eyes make me drunk enough." Patrick wrapped his arms around her once again. Helen melted into his chest.

"Tell me more."

"The bedrooms will be upstairs—one on each side—same size as the rooms below. You can pick which one will be ours, either above the big room or above the kitchen. We'll keep the cradle in our room—and we'll keep it full."

"Spoken like the Irish rogue that you are Mr. O'Bierne."

"Then, as they get older, they'll move across the way, into the other bedroom."

"It all sounds so wonderful."

"You'll have rock chimneys on each end of the house. A big one for the kitchen, because it will be used for cooking and heating, and a good-sized one for the other end of the house."

Patrick looked toward the distant mountain. He found it easy to imagine what it would be like once completed. He could even see smoke curling from the double chimneys on a crisp autumn evening.

"I've already bartered with Mr. Johnston. He's a good stonemason. He will build our chimneys good and tall, so they will draw easy. And he'll line them with clay, and fire them so they're glazed smooth as glass."

Patrick and Helen had witnessed the result of poorly made fireplaces back in the Five Points. Tenants burned whatever was cheap or readily at hand. Seasoned wood was purchased at a premium resulting in scrap lumber and trash being the most common heating material.

These materials didn't burn cleanly, leaving behind a thick layer of creosote coating the stovepipes and flues. On one occasion this creosote buildup had burst into flames inside a chimney, creating a fire much like a blast furnace.

The excessive heat of the runaway fire ignited the wood surrounding the chimney. A city block was consumed before the blaze was brought under control. In that one fire, the O'Brien's lost six adult friends and their combined twelve children.

"What did you barter with?"

"I'm swapping out his labor for some milled lumber."

"That's good."

"And your house will have two big, wide porches. One front and back. Each will be eight feet wide and run the length of the house."

"A porch front and back?"

Helen turned to look into his face. Her green eyes went wide as she teased. "You mean we won't have dirt floors?"

"Your house will have wooden floors and it will be up off the ground. I'll put the flooring joists up on stacked rock pilings. That way I can make the floor level. The chickens will be able to work in under the house, eating termites and ticks."

"I hope they get all the ticks."

"I'll check you regular for any they miss."

"Quit."

"And since you don't want Connell's puppy in the house..."

"No, I don't!"

"It'll give him and the other dogs a cool place to lie during the summer days, and a warm, dry spot when it's snowing or raining." Patrick continued, "And a place to come boiling out of when company shows up. Especially uninvited company."

"Don't run off all my company," Helen smiled.

"And the floor won't be cherry puncheon either. It will be made with an oak under-floor, covered with milled black walnut."

"Black walnut...that will be beautiful."

"Aye. First, I'll lay down the oak floor—then I'll put down the walnut, crosswise. That'll seal up any cracks old man winter's fingers might find. With wet sand and wooden blocks, I'll scrub the walnut smooth, so bare feet won't find any splinters."

"You have sure given this a lot of thought."

"I think about it every minute of every day."

Helen kissed him gently on the mouth. "It'll be a grand home!" Helen breathed in a long, slow breath. "A grand home indeed."

By the end of the summer, Patrick had completed Helen's home. It was a house to be proud of—sturdy and well built. It stood two stories tall against the backdrop of mountains and evergreens. Glass windows, special ordered and shipped from Little Rock, looked out on the world while offering a glimpse into the heart of a family. Wide porches smiled a warm welcome to visitors and customers alike. This was a family home, but it was also an advertisement for the neighbors.

Patrick was indeed a master carpenter. He would begin his legacy by milling lumber, then transforming that lumber into rugged, sturdy homes in this new land. Homes that could withstand all Mother Nature could throw at them while keeping those inside warm and safe.

His own home completed, Patrick kept his promise to Hans and Elizabeth. He immediately set about cutting timber for their home. The Göbel's had been living in a wagon since they'd moved onto their property. It had a strong canvas cover and was off the ground, out of the way of crawling things, but it wasn't a home.

Hans had busied himself by planting and tending his grapevines. Still, he'd found time to help Patrick. He had a few *civilized* ideas of his own, which he'd suggested in the construction of the O'Brien's home. Like a firebox next to the fireplaces that could be filled from outside and accessed from within the house without having to go out in the weather to fetch wood.

Hans and Patrick worked together, or at least talked every week. Therefore, Hans didn't think it necessary to build a temporary log cabin. Patrick had promised him a fine home of their own before the first snow. Hans never once gave it a second thought. Patrick would keep his word.

In the fall of 1833, well before the leaves turned their riot of fall color, both families were in sturdy homes. And on October 3rd, Elizabeth Göbel was called upon for her skills as a midwife.

Helen O'Brien gave birth to a baby boy. It was the first baby born into the valley since the two families had arrived. They named him Killian.

11

The week before Killian's birth, Hans was on his way home with a loaded wagon of fresh-cut lumber. On the return trip from the O'Brien's mill in Cliffy Hollow, he'd hit the main road down the banks of Little Piney and then turned up the trail on Devil's Fork. It was the quickest and smoothest way to get to his house on Owen's Creek. It also required him to pass both of the Ranklins' places. Nearing Benjamin and Sarah's cabin, he spotted a bare-chested mountain man chopping firewood beside his cabin.

Sweat glistened on the bunched muscles of the man's hairy back as the ax bit deeply into the log. An explosion of chips arched into the surrounding grass with each strike.

"Hail, Ben."

"Hello yourself."

Ranklin arched the ax up again, slamming its sharp head into the log once more with a solid thump. Again there was an explosion of wood chips. Straightening up, he wiped sweat from his forehead before looking over at his neighbor.

"Didn't mean to sneak up on you," Hans said.

Ranklin snorted a laugh. "Didn't know you could be so funny Göbel," he said.

"What did I say that was funny?"

"All the blooming racket you'us making with that loaded wagon," he said. "I heard you coming a mile away. Indians would have lifted my scalp years ago if I couldn't hear any better than that."

"Well, we don't have to worry about Indians these days."

"Depends on the Indian." Benjamin swung the double-bitted ax one-handed in a large loop. With a solid thump, the shiny blade sunk deep into the top of a block of wood. Leaving it there to prevent rusting, he brushed at his leather britches before picking up a small jug. Hooking the index finger of his right hand in the circular hole in the neck, he flipped the jug onto his crooked forearm and lifted the mouth of the jug to his parched lips.

"Care for a taste?" he asked as he lowered the jug.

"Just a short one," Hans replied.

Everyone knew it was bad manners to refuse to drink with a man. Anyway, Hans never missed a chance to compare the product of other men against his own.

"Not as good as what you make," Benjamin admitted. "But it's wet."

Ben walked closer to the road. That way he wouldn't have to shout to carry on a conversation. He handed the jug up to Hans.

Hans took a short pull at the jug. He screwed up his face at the bitter taste.

"What's in it?" he said. "If you don't mind my asking."

"Naw, I don't mind." Benjamin Ranklin tilted his head and winked. "It's a recipe I learned during my Indian trading days. You take an empty ten-gallon whiskey barrel. Put in three-gallon of alcohol for a base. Chunk in a handful of red Spanish peppers. Add one-pound of black twist tobacco for color, and a pound of molasses for smoothing. You'll need six gallons of

Arkansas River water. You could use Little Piney water, but you need to collect it at flood stage. And then you throw in two rattlesnake heads for bite."

With a grimace, Hans looked at Benjamin with one eye closed. "I think it's still a mite green," he said. "Probably needs a scorpion or two."

Both men laughed as Hans handed the jug back.

"See you been helping Irish again," Benjamin said.

"Been over that way. Got some more lumber for my outbuildings."

Pitch still oozed from the fresh-cut planks. It gave the air around the wagon a harsh smell of turpentine that was sharp to the nose.

"Making himself right at home in my hollow I hear," Benjamin said. "Damned the crick and all."

Hans ignored the first half of Ranklin's statement. There was no need to beat a dead horse. No matter what he said, Ranklin wasn't going to let it go.

"He's got a nice sawmill going," Hans said.

"Best enjoy it whilst he can," Benjamin said.

"Damned the creek, built a nice mill race for the water to run, and set up a water wheel to run the saw," Hans said. "Cuts a lot smoother and quicker than using the pit method. You should have him cut you some lumber for a house."

"Something wrong with my cabin?" Ranklin asked.

Both men glanced across the trail at the makeshift cabin. Large sections between the cottonwood logs were missing globs of chinking. It was obvious that winter would find entry points.

"That's not what I meant."

Hans didn't want to hurt Benjamin's feelings, but the

dirt floor cabin had been built with gum and cottonwood logs. Both were softwood and would rot quickly.

"We both know them logs won't last many winters," Hans said.

"It'll last well enough."

Benjamin looked at his cabin as if seeing it for the first time. He'd thrown it together with little thought of permanence. The softer woods had been lighter to stack and easier to notch on the ends and around the doorway. Mud and grass had served as his chinking material. That too would need extensive repair before winter took too strong a grip.

"Ain't fancy," he said. "But it's enough."

"What about when things turn cold?" Hans asked.

The storm in Ranklin's eyes seemed to subside as he realized Hans wasn't trying to insult him. At least he didn't seem to be taking the conversation as a challenge.

"Spent many a winter in a hide teepee," he continued, "with nothing more than a squaw and a buffalo robe to keep me warm."

"What about your brother?" Hans asked.

"Don't think I'd like to spend a winter under a buffalo robe with him."

Benjamin made the statement as dry as an August dust storm. Only a sparkle in his black eyes gave the joke away. It was probably the first time Hans had seen those dark eyes when they weren't brooding or dead.

"Neither would I."

Hans tried to keep a straight face but couldn't. He busted out with a good belly laugh. It took him a few minutes, and another pull on the jug, to get back around to his original question.

"I mean, do you think Jacob would need some building material?"

"I think he's satisfied with what he's got," Benjamin said. "You'd need to ask him direct."

Jacob had found an overhanging slate bluff near his brother's cabin. It had a level undercut area that reached back about fifteen feet. A well-used fire pit indicated the spot had been used as temporary shelter by foraging hunters for generations.

Jacob and his wife, Priscilla, had built their hovel by dry stacking loose rocks across the opening until it was nearly closed off. This created their outer walls. With poles and hides, he left one opening for a door. He didn't stack rocks to the top, but left a small slit open, where the rock wall and the slate overhang nearly met. This was for smoke to escape. Jacob expected his wife and kids to make do, living in this manmade cave.

Hans had passed by the spot many times as he moved about the valley. The only people working to try to improve their lot at Jacob's place were his wife and children. Unlike Benjamin, Jacob didn't even split the firewood.

The communal Ranklin garden was the same thing, Sarah and Priscilla had to work that alone. Their only help was from the children. Priscilla had even ended up doing most of the work on the shelter by herself. Jacob and Benjamin were usually off rambling or commercial hunting for the various taverns and Inns along the Arkansas River. Ducks, pigeons, elk, and buffalo were in constant demand. Word was that the two brothers were making a decent living.

"Think Jacob might need some lumber?" Hans asked.

"I'm not my brother's keeper," Benjamin said. "Jacob takes care of his own."

"I'll ask him then," Hans said.

"How come you're drumming up business for Irish?" Benjamin asked. "You his partner now or something?"

"Just trying to help my neighbors," Hans replied. "Patrick could use the business and I figured you might need the lumber."

"If I did," Benjamin snapped, "it wouldn't be from a thief."

12

The morning of November 13, 1833, started differently from any other. Helen O'Brien was expecting a child any day now, and the Göbel's had overslept. Something they never did.

"Hans. Get up," Elizabeth said. "We've laid in past sunup."

"Are you out of your mind woman?"

"Come on now. Shake them covers," she said. "We're late. I've got to get over to Helen's. That young'un will be here any time now."

Hans' pocket watch lay open on the stand next to the bed. He looked at the face to discover it clearly showed three o'clock.

"According to my watch," he said. "We've two more hours before we need to get up."

"Either your watch is wrong, or the house is on fire," Elizabeth said. "Look how bright it is outside."

Hans looked at the bedroom window and saw that Elizabeth was right. Light poured in at the window as if the morning was half gone. Something strange was afoot.

Rising quickly from bed, he padded over to the window and looked out. The sky itself appeared to be on fire. Brilliant fireballs filled the heavens, shooting in every direction, trailed by comet-like tails.

"Come here old woman," Hans called. "Either it's an early snow and the snowflakes are on fire or we're having a humdinger of a meteor shower."

Elizabeth joined him at the window. "Have you ever in your life," she said.

Hundreds of streaking meteors zipped across the night sky. They had both seen shooting stars before, but never more than a handful in an entire hour. If these had been snowflakes as Hans had first said, it would be two feet deep in half an hour.

"Just look how bright!"

"I've never seen anything like this," he began to chuckle.

"What's so funny?"

"I was just thinking about how busy the preacher's gonna be."

"Preacher?"

"It's the end of the world," Hans laughed out loud. "Think how many folks he's gonna have to baptize today."

"Oh, will you hush," Elizabeth couldn't help but smile. "I don't know if Wednesday, November the 13th, 1833, is the end of the world or not, but I bet that baby comes today!"

"Then we'd better get you over there," Hans said.

"See if we're the only ones privileged to seeing the world end."

Chuckling to himself, Hans turned and walked over to his clothes. He had left them piled up in a straight-backed chair near the foot of the bed. Sitting on the edge of the bed, he began to pull on his britches and a stiff new pair of brogans.

"I'll start breakfast," Elizabeth called back over her shoulder. She was already three steps down the stairs when Hans looked up.

It was well past sunrise when the Göbel's wagon rumbled into the O'Brien's front yard. As Hans tied the mule to the cedar tree next to the front porch, he looked up at a sky still saturated with meteors. Patrick and Connell were sitting on the edge of the porch, Connell's short legs dangling in space.

"Elizabeth thinks today's the day," Hans said.

"Helen thinks so, too," Patrick replied.

"Looks like somebody up there's celebrating a little early. Hope they're all correct in their assumptions."

"Well, Connell," Hans placed one foot on the porch and leaned toward the boy. "What do you think of all these fireworks?"

"It's purty," Connell giggled.

"Purty, pretty much says it all," Hans agreed.

"We've been watching it for hours," Patrick said gently patting his son on the back.

"Helen even got out of bed to watch for a while."

Elizabeth marched on in through the open door into the kitchen after giving Connell a hug and a little kiss on the cheek. Looking around she didn't see any sign of dirty dishes or freshly cooked food.

"You haven't fixed her or that boy any breakfast yet," she scolded. "Have you?"

"Helen ain't hungry," Patrick laughed. "And Connell always is."

"Well, I'll fix 'em both something they can get down." Elizabeth rattled pans and opened cabinet doors.

"Get upstairs and let Helen know I'm here," she ordered.

"As much racket as you're making," Hans threw his dog into the hunt, "I think she already knows that."

"Hans Göbel! Don't you start sassing me." There was a smile in Elizabeth's voice. "It'd be a terrible thing for young Connell to see a grown man get his britches warmed."

Hans and Patrick nodded knowingly to each other as Connell giggled. The two men decided they'd better make themselves scarce for a while. Patrick stood and let Connell jump from the porch onto his back. The three headed down to the creek and the mill. While Connell threw rocks in the middle of the backed-up pond, Patrick and Hans sampled some of Hans' special recipe.

Eventually, they made their way back up the hill and to Connell's breakfast. While Elizabeth fussed over him in the kitchen, the two men moved outside under the cedar tree. Hunkering down on the soft ground, they sipped frequently from a small jug and discussed the ways of nature. They were just waiting to be needed.

"Talked with Ben Ranklin the other day," Hans said.

"And how's my sweetheart doing?" Patrick quipped.

"I wish you two could get together on this thing," Hans passed the jug back. "This feud isn't good for either of you or the valley."

"I'm not the one with a problem." Patrick pulled a long draw from the jug. "He's the one making accusations and calling names."

"But you should be the better man," Hans pleaded. "You could make the effort to end it."

"How?" Patrick looked Hans squarely in the face. "You suggesting I move out and give him this hollow?"

"I'm not saying that."

"What then?" Patrick took another swallow. "He claims I stole this hollow from him," he said. "And he wants it back. Nothing short of that is going to satisfy him."

"There ought to be some middle ground somewhere."

"The only ground he's interested in, other than this hollow, is a six-by-six plot under a cedar tree." Patrick picked up a handful of dirt and sifted it through his fingers. "He wants me in it. With plenty of dirt on top."

"You're probably right."

"I'll be as civil as I can to that entire Ranklin clan," Patrick's voice hardened. "But when push comes to shove, before I give up my home, it'll be him they're patting dirt on."

Before anything else could be said, Elizabeth called from upstairs.

"Patrick O'Brien! You'd best get up here."

Patrick ran inside and climbed the stairs to the upper bedroom where Helen lay. As he entered the bedroom, he found his wife heavy into labor.

"You're about to be a papa," Elizabeth said.

Shortly after noon, Patrick was holding a brand-new son.

"He don't weigh no more than a large fox squirrel," Patrick said.

"He is a mite on the light side," Elizabeth said.

As if in protest to the discussion on his size, the baby began to cry. The sound quickly reached an ear-piercing crescendo.

"Don't like daddy talking about the boy, do you?" Helen said as she reached for her newest child.

From downstairs, Hans called out, "What ya'll birthing up there, babies or Hereford bulls?"

The day began with celestial fireworks. All of America would remember the day because of the meteoric phenomenon. Even the Indians would refer to it as the night the *stars fell from the sky*. But the O'Brien's would remember, and celebrate, the birth of Killian O'Brien.

13

"I knew this baby would be here today," Elizabeth beamed.

"And he's such a fine, stout, young fellow. Just look at him grip my finger."

"Would you and Hans be my baby's godparents?" an exhausted Helen asked.

"Our feelings would be hurt if you hadn't asked."

Elizabeth lifted the little bundle in her arms.

"What are you going to name him?"

"We'll call him Killian."

"Welcome to Arkansas, Killian O'Brien."

Elizabeth's face glowed. She was thrilled to help bring this new life into the territory—especially since it was the child of her dearest friend—and her godchild.

It was mid-November when Helen gave birth. The newest O'Brien greeted his Ozark home in one of the upstairs bedrooms. Outside, on the hillsides and creek banks, hickory and sweet gum were beginning to change, already flush with their riot of fall colors. The morning air held a cool bite until mid-day. That night, Cliffy Hollow's rugged peaks heard the first lonesome honk of geese winging south.

"We're reminded of the balance."

Elizabeth sat drinking coffee at the kitchen table with Hans and Patrick. Connell was already asleep from his busy day. Helen and Killian were resting comfortably upstairs. While outside, the meteor shower continued again with nightfall, but to a much lesser degree. Elizabeth poured coffee into a saucer and then blew across its surface to cool it before she continued. "With life comes death."

"What do you mean?" Patrick asked. "Is there something wrong with Helen or Killian?"

"Oh no," Elizabeth said, "just talking about winter coming."

Patrick wasn't sure he believed she was telling him the truth. There was something more on her mind. Had she seen a sign, or had a dream? Something was eating at her, but unless she decided to share it, there was no way to know what it might be. If she was trying to tell him something he needed to know, he wished she'd just come right out and say it.

"Guess you'll be headed home now?" Patrick asked.

"No," Elizabeth said. "I'll stick around for a couple of days. Our new baby and mother might need me."

Patrick wanted to take Elizabeth's statement for what it was. She was staying to be with her friend and new baby. Nothing more. That was the way things would be—it was not a request. She would sleep in the other upstairs bedroom to be close to her charges. But the way she said, 'they might need me,' gave him pause.

"You and Connell sleep downstairs," she said. "Hans will just have to go back home and fend for himself until I get back."

For the next few days, Elizabeth helped with the cooking and cleaning until Helen was up and about. She insisted that little Killian and Helen might need her. And if they did, you could bet that she was going to be right there. It wasn't necessary. Patrick could handle the mill and whatever house chores needed doing. But there was no way either Patrick or Hans were going to convince Elizabeth otherwise. Both men knew better than to try.

After the birth of Killian, things seemed to settle into a routine. Over the next few years, more and more settlers filtered into the valley. First, they needed help from the O'Brien's, cutting and milling lumber, then turning that into a home. The next most common event would be their calling on the Göbel's for Elizabeth's skills as a mid-wife.

These happy times required Hans' special skills. Whether it was a barn raising, moving into a new home, or the birth of a new member of the community, Han's wine and his skill at brewing beer was well received. If things were dull for too long a stretch, Patrick could come up with something special to celebrate all on his own.

There were somber times also. Sometimes there would be complications with a birth, and a couple of the babies were lost. Twice babies were stillborn. One of the stillborn children belonged to Jacob and Priscilla Ranklin. No one blamed Elizabeth for the tragedies, no one that is except Jacob Ranklin.

"That old witch," Jacob had said. "She put a spell on Priscilla. She ain't had no trouble with any of the others."

Patrick had seen Elizabeth agonize for days over each loss, especially the Ranklin child. Life was precious to her. And Jacob's vile tongue just added to the hatred brewing between Patrick and the Ranklin clan.

Of all the complicated births and deaths in the valley, of all the gifts and losses, one birth upset Elizabeth more than any other.

Patrick remembered Elizabeth telling him and Helen all about it. It happened a year after the birth of Killian. It was a birth where everything went right. There were no complications. There were no problems. No troubles. The birth was easy. Too easy.

That, along with the signs accompanying the birth, shook Elizabeth to her core. That was the birth of Benjamin and Sarah Ranklin's first child. The birth of Caleb Ranklin.

14

"Mrs. Göbel! Mrs. Göbel!"

Someone was trying to pound the door off its hinges.

"Are you home?"

Hans, shotgun in hand, cautiously swung the door open to a pasty-faced Benjamin Ranklin.

"What in thunder's the cause of this ruckus?"

The mountain man couldn't stand still. Fidgeting like a nervous schoolboy about to be whipped, he shifted his weight from foot to foot. Behind him, a half-dozen of the Göbel's dogs, teeth bared, spittle flecking their mouths, growled, chopped, and barked at the intruder.

"You'd think these dogs had treed the devil himself!"

Benjamin ignored Hans when he saw Elizabeth standing back inside the room. He swiped his hat off and dropped his head as if to apologize for some wrong. He directed his question directly to her as he twisted his fur hat until it looked like something the dogs had wallowed into a ball. It was evident he was upset about something, and it wasn't the dogs.

"Mrs. Göbel, we need your help."

The swarm of yapping dogs continued to circle just beyond reach. They'd formed a semi-circle with Benjamin as the point of interest. Ears laid back, their mouths chopped at the air. They wanted to rush in and bite, but there was something about the man that convinced them they'd better not try.

"Hush up there! Hush it up!" Elizabeth scolded the dogs as she stepped into the doorway, pushing past her husband and out onto the porch. "What on earth is the matter, Mr. Ranklin?" She reached out and took his hand.

"You're shaking like you got a fever."

"It's Sarah...I think it's her time...can you come?"

"Mercy sakes!" It was Elizabeth's turn to become animated. "I feared she'd be early."

"Priscilla's there with her right now," Benjamin tripped over his words. "I came to fetch you as quick as I could."

"Get on back home and tell her I'm on my way!"

Elizabeth wheeled around to start gathering her things. She was confronted again by the spectacle of Hans standing in the middle of the floor wearing nothing but his nightshirt, a shotgun in his hands.

"Just let me get a few things, Benjamin," she called over her shoulder, "and I'll be right there. Hans. Hitch up the buggy. It's Sarah."

Benjamin Ranklin turned, wading through the pack of hounds, oblivious to their existence. The circuit preacher would have thought it reminiscent of Moses parting the Red Sea.

One black-and-tan made the mistake of getting too close. For his effort he received a well-placed kick to the side of the head. The dog tucked his tail between his legs, cowed his head and pissed on the ground. He knew there was a more dangerous predator than he on the prod. The black and tan hound whimpered and whined as he slunk back underneath the front porch. The rest of the pack fell momentarily silent.

Ranklin swung up into the saddle and wheeled the mare with a sharp jab in her flank. The horse sprang into action. Hooves throwing up a small cloud of dust and loose dirt, they were off. The sight of the mare escaping gave one of the dogs courage. Finding its voice once again, he boiled out after her. A caravan of a yapping dog, horse and rider, were soon around the bend and out of sight.

Elizabeth rushed about getting her things ready. Hans jerked off his nightshirt, slid on his pants and shirt then stabbed his feet into his brogans. Clomping out the front door, he headed for the barn to hitch up the wagon.

Putting on his jacket as he went, it looked as if he was being attacked. Arms flapping overhead, the jacket swirling around his head, it gave the appearance of a man being flogged by some strange bird. Stabbing his hands at the armholes of the jacket, he was nearly winning the battle as he entered the barn door.

Hans' preoccupation with the jacket didn't slow him down much. In record time he had the mule hitched and was pulling up to the porch.

"Ready?" he called out.

In the house, Elizabeth double-checked everything in her little bag. She was just shutting the front door as Hans pulled up.

"Just keep your shirt on." Elizabeth stepped down from the porch. Reaching up to take Hans' extended hand; she climbed up onto the wagon seat.

"A person would think *you* were being called on," Elizabeth jabbed. "The way you're trying to rush me around."

It was evident that Elizabeth was concerned about this turn of events. An early baby was never a good thing, but especially not today. She took her agitation out on Hans because he was a convenient target.

"Once we get there, you'll just be sitting around twiddling your thumbs." Elizabeth poked her agitation in her husband's direction. "We women folk will be doing all the work, as usual."

"Some truth in that."

Hans knew Elizabeth wasn't upset with him. Still, he didn't care for the tongue lashing.

"But it's me you depend on to get you there ain't it?" He could feel the upsetting undercurrent. He, too, was upset, and he wanted the last word, even if it was 'yes mam.'

The trip to the Ranklin cabin took half an hour. Plenty of time for Hans and Elizabeth to talk. The strange timing of the birth nagged at Hans. He wanted to voice his concerns—wanted to talk about it—but wasn't sure how to approach the subject.

"Think Sarah'll be all right?"

"She'll be all right." There was an edge in Elizabeth's voice that said she wasn't sure. Concern was one thing Elizabeth could never hide. Not from the man who had lived with her most of her life.

"That lady's tough as a hickory sapling." Elizabeth paused before continuing, "I'd be lying if I said I weren't concerned about her age—this being her first child and all."

"You know I'm not talking about her years," Hans said what they were both thinking. Benjamin Ranklin was fifty-seven and Sarah was thirty-three. Sarah had been married once before, but neither that marriage nor this one had produced any children.

Now here she was, late in life, and having a baby. It had been a shock to most in the valley, and common gossip at every dance, picnic or Sunday meeting. But advanced age was not what was eating at the Göbel's.

"Talking about the signs and you know it."

"Baby might come before..." Elizabeth's voice trailed off, "...or maybe after."

The wagon bounced over a melon-sized rock, jarring them both. Although it wasn't Han's driving that bothered her, Elizabeth lashed out. "Watch where you're going!"

Hans ignored her complaint. Shaking his head, he snapped the reins and clucked to the mule. "Not good, I tell you," he said. "Got me a bad feeling about all this."

"So do I," Elizabeth admitted. "So do I."

For the next few minutes, neither of them said a word. It was Elizabeth who finally broke the silence. "But there's nothing we can do about it," she said. "It's all in the Lord's hands."

"So mote it be," Hans whispered. "So mote it be."

They rode the rest of the way without the benefit of conversation. Jostling down the rough trail beside Devil's Fork, Elizabeth was lost in her thoughts. Hans continued to mutter to himself about it being the devil's day.

Nearly as often as they read the Bible, the Göbel's read the *Old Farmer's Almanac*. Like most people, they used it for when to plant, when to harvest, and when to cut hogs. With the pamphlet, you could study the signs of the zodiac. You wouldn't want to plant a root crop when the signs were in the head or arms, it would never grow any tubers, only leaves.

The Göbel's also used it for information on celestial movements and weather. From their study, they knew that on November 30, 1834, there would be a total eclipse of the sun.

Hans and Elizabeth had brought more than grapevines and doctoring skills from the old country. They'd brought their culture, their legends, and their superstitions.

The celestial gyrations were more than wives' tales about an owl hooting during the middle of the day portending someone's death. They carried more weight than the way a spider spun its webs or how wooly a caterpillar was. This was a powerful warning.

Pitch black in the middle of the day and the possibility of a birth, right in the middle of that. Celestial warnings like this should be heeded.

The Göbel's had more formal education than their neighbors. They knew about the physical revolutions of the planets. They understood there was a rhyme and reason for everything. It was a delicate balance. Good versus evil—light versus dark. A balance dictated by higher powers.

The greater of those powers was light. That power resided with the Great Architect of the Universe. The designer of all things great and small. He'd laid out just how things should be. How it should be with the balance leaning toward good.

But in the cosmic struggle, there was a dark side too. Satan. Satan and his chief angel, Beelzebub. These demons had powers too, and they used them. And those powers were dark.

According to Germanic legend, an eclipse is caused when Beelzebub turns his hell-wolf loose to devour the sun. In the resulting darkness, out of God's sight, the devil can call forth the dead and the undead. They walk the earth doing his bidding. An eclipse is a time for garlic and silver bullets. It is a time for prayers.

The Göbel's knew this. But the Ranklin's had no idea of what was coming. They didn't know to expect the eclipse nor to expect the evil that would accompany it.

The way things were shaping up, this birth could very well coincide with the eclipse. And this was not just a glancing partial eclipse. Oh, no. This would be a total eclipse. The devil would be in the fullness of his power.

15

As soon as they arrived at the Ranklin's cabin, Elizabeth hustled inside. Sarah's sister-in-law, Priscilla Ranklin, was already there. She had a kettle of water boiling in the fireplace.

"Sarah's over there."

Benjamin pointed to a rope bed in the corner of the cramped room. Sarah's spare body was nearly lost in a pile of buffalo robes and fox pelts.

"She doesn't seem to be in much pain," offered Priscilla.

"Sarah's going to be all right, Benjamin," Elizabeth reassured him. "You get outside and let us do our work."

"Ben," Han's placed a hand on Ben's broad shoulder. "You might as well come away from there."

Leading his charge toward the woodpile, Hans tried to comfort his neighbor. Sometimes these things seemed to be worse on the father than the mother.

"The womenfolk will take care of everything—could be awhile though—might as well get comfortable. Let's sit and whittle."

Elizabeth and Priscilla began preparing for the birth. Few of the valley settlers had ever seen a real town doctor, even in passing. Folk remedies and granny ladies met all their needs.

"Shore am glad you're here," Priscilla whispered. "Things always go better when you're around."

Elizabeth cleared off the table and rolled out a clean towel to place her things on. She glanced at the too lean form lying on the pile of hides on the bed. Hopefully, this one would go well.

"I've been mid-wife to most of the births in this valley," she said. "We've been lucky not to lose any more than we have."

Realizing what she'd said, Elizabeth's face reddened. Priscilla continued to fiddle with the pot of water she'd swung over the fire as if nothing had been said. The memory of delivering a stillborn girl to Priscilla came rushing back to embarrass Elizabeth. She was certain that was what Priscilla was also remembering. A hurt that deep is forever raw to a mother.

"I'm sorry about your little girl," Elizabeth said. "But there was nothing I could do. The precious little thing never had a chance."

"That weren't your fault," she said.

"Your husband seems to think it was."

Priscilla turned to face Elizabeth. Both women looked into each other's eyes for a long moment. A shared tenderness passed between the two hurts.

"We both know it weren't," Priscilla finally said. "If it were anybody's fault, it were mine," she continued. "I should'a watched what I was doing."

"I blame Jacob," Elizabeth said. "There you were, big with child, and he was off gallivanting. He should have been doing that plowing instead of you and the kids."

The incident had taken place in the spring. Jacob had been off commercial hunting and doing a little light stealing when he should have been home. Before he'd left, he told Priscilla he expected her and the kids to have a new garden spot broke and cleared by the time he got back. The new ground was full of large rocks. Every time the plow point struck a rock, the plow would stop suddenly and jerk sideways. With each jerk, the wooden plow handles struck her a vicious blow. By the end of the day, the sides of her expanded stomach were bruised.

"Jacob told me to be careful afore he left," Priscilla said. "It were my fault."

"But that's why you lost the baby," Elizabeth said.

"I knew exactly when she quit moving inside me," Priscilla said. "If you hadn't got there when you did," there was a short pause. "I might not have made it either."

Elizabeth eased closer to Priscilla. She reached over and patted Priscilla's forearm. With moistened eyes, she enveloped her in a warm hug. "I'm sorry," she whispered.

16

It took a few minutes for the women to regain their composure and to return to the task at hand.

"Here," Elizabeth was the first to speak. "Let's get some lanterns lit. We'll need more light. This cabin is too dark."

There was only one window and it was dim in the little cabin. It was obvious they could use more light. Elizabeth didn't say anything about expecting it to get much darker. She didn't want to scare the two women.

Elizabeth laid out the rest of her equipment. She'd brought her good scissors, some waxed thread, and a stout needle. For quilling, she had a turkey feather and some cayenne pepper. In case the mother tried to fight the contractions, she could blow some of the pepper up her nose, making her sneeze. It would help push the baby out.

There was castor oil to help induce labor and evening primrose oil to ease the baby's exit. She also had salt, baking soda, and honey to make a potion in case the mother became sick and started vomiting. Last, she reached deep into her bag and brought out a garland of garlic. This she placed near the head of the bed.

"What's with the garlic?" Priscilla asked as she swung the pot of water back over the fire. "That's a new one on me. I don't remember garlic being used at any of my deliveries, and I've had a passel of 'em. Is it something new?"

"It helps cover the smell." Elizabeth tried to act as if it was something she normally did. "Sometimes helps to rub some on the cord after I cut it, too. Cuts down on fever. You probably just didn't notice it before."

Out in the yard, Hans tried to occupy Benjamin's mind with talk of everything from crops to trapping.

"Shore like this knife for whittling," Hans said. "Fits my hand."

The oldest Ranklin was having a tough time paying attention. Every little sound escaping from the cabin had him springing to his feet like a jack-in-the-box.

"What was that? Did you hear that? Wonder what that was?"

"Just relax," Hans soothed. "They'll call you when it's here. If'n you don't start paying attention to your whittling, you're gonna cut your arm clean off. Then you'll be the one needing doctoring— 'stead of Sarah."

Benjamin just couldn't sit still. Pacing back and forth, he was an agitated bear caught in a trap he couldn't figure out. "How long does this usually take?"

"Never can tell," Hans said. "Sometimes they come right away and sometimes they want to wait."

"At her age, this is dangerous ain't it?" Benjamin wrung his hands together, not knowing what to do with his useless appendages.

"Everything in these hills is dangerous," Han's said. "Sarah'll do just fine."

"I mean dangerous for the kid!" He'd stopped pacing and was looking proudly at Hans. "It's going to be a boy! I just know it!" Then his face became dark and brooding. "At least it best be!" His voice trailed off. "Elsewise, they'll be hell to pay."

The realization hit Hans like a punch in the gut. The look on Ben's face told it all. He could care less about Sarah's chances. As long as she delivered him a healthy son, nothing else mattered. Especially not Sarah.

Until now, Hans had naturally thought the man was worried about his wife. All the gossips had focused on Sarah's age and how difficult everyone expected the birth to be. Most were concerned that she might not survive the ordeal. Tongues had wagged that even tough ol' Ben was concerned about his wife's chances.

"Why just the other day I saw ol' Ben and Sarah over at Hagarville," the gossip had offered. "He was helping her down from the wagon like she was made out of china or something."

"Who would have ever thought that he had feelings for anybody," another had added.

"That old buzzard is dedicated to her, I tell you," said another.

Now, the truth was finally exposed. Benjamin Ranklin expected Sarah to bring him a son. That was what he had been protecting. If she died in the process, so be it. Hans wondered how he'd react if Sarah survived and the child didn't? Or what if Sarah delivered a girl?

"Ben, you're pacing like a mountain lion on a rope." Long curls of pine slid from Hans' knife. There was enough tinder around his feet to start a dozen morning cook fires. "Sit yourself down and whittle," Hans said. "It'll get your mind off'n it for a while."

"Fighting Indians is easier than this," Benjamin muttered. He sat down heavily. Taking off his hat, he placed it on his knee. Reaching up with both hands, he ran them through his graying hair. Hans could see that he was sweating.

"First born's sometimes rougher on the pa than it is on the ma," Hans chuckled. "Just sit a spell. You're going to wear them boots clean out."

Priscilla came to the cabin door.

"Her time is getting closer," she said. "It won't be long now."

As if on cue, the light began to fade.

17

"What the...?" the dimming light surprised Benjamin Ranklin. "Am I going blind?"

"Eclipse is starting." Hans took out a silver-plated pocket watch. Popping open the cover, he looked at the intricate Swiss face. The watch showed eleven-thirty.

"Eclipse?"

"There's supposed to be an eclipse of the sun today."

"Ain't that a devilish thing...?" Benjamin's focus shifted from the sky back to the cabin door.

The failing light brought with it a physical weight, as if a giant hand pressed down on the world, making it harder to breathe. The Göbel's mule, still hitched to the wagon, nickered and began to paw at the ground. Chickens, thinking it nightfall, scurried across the yard. Flapping their wings noisily, they flew up into the elm tree to roost. From somewhere not too far up Devil's Fork, a panther screamed in defiance. Small birds stopped flitting in the bushes and became quiet. Darkness slowly devoured the world. The only light visible leaked from inside the cabin.

It took an hour-and-a-half for the world to go from the promise of a bright noon time to dark midnight. Total darkness lasted only a minute before it began to creep back toward light. But in the heart of the darkest moment, a cold wind wrapped Hans in its clammy grip. Hans felt it through to the marrow of his bones.

It was precisely at that moment that a cry shattered the stillness. The baby had arrived. Hans struck a match and looked at his watch again—twelve fifty-five.

Inside the cabin, Elizabeth was prepared. Lantern light fought against the pitch-black from the outside. It bathed the inside of the cabin with a warm glow. But even close to the warm of the lanterns, Elizabeth too felt the chill that gripped her husband. Darkness ruled the world. A blind person could have felt it.

Sarah's last contraction had begun with the eclipse. Halfway through the eclipse, the baby's head had crowned. To Sarah and Priscilla, it all seemed to be quite natural. Only Elizabeth seemed to notice the ease with which everything took place.

Once Sarah felt the first twinge of a contraction, she had just begun to bear down, and suddenly, the baby was in this world.

In the returning light, Benjamin and Hans made their way into the cabin. Entering the room, they saw Priscilla moving toward the fireplace to fetch more warm water. Elizabeth was wiping the baby with a cloth, cleaning the slime from his eyes and mouth. She turned in time to see the men enter the room. Hans noticed her shoulders seemed to droop as she turned back around and placed the baby on its mother's chest.

"Well...?" asked the new father.

"It's a boy!" Priscilla shouted, not able to contain her joy.

"Your wife and son are doing fine," Elizabeth added.

There was a tenseness to her tone that only Hans noticed.

Benjamin Ranklin directed his statement to Hans. "I told you it'd be a boy." As an afterthought, he turned to Elizabeth for reassurance. "And he's going to be all right?"

"Yes," Elizabeth said. "He's doing just fine. Come look at him."

"Come see your new son," Sarah said.

He moved slowly to the side of the bed, careful not to make too much noise. Sarah looked drained and exhausted, but there was a broad smile on her face. She pulled the covers back to expose the face of Benjamin's new pride.

"I don't know what all the fuss was about," Sarah said. "He just squirted out like a melon seed between your fingers."

"No, she didn't have any problems," Elizabeth admitted. "Everything went smooth as sweet milk."

"Well, Indian squaws do it all the time," Benjamin said. "Just go off by themselves and come back with a baby. Can't be much to it."

Elizabeth fumed at Ranklin's lack of compassion for his wife. All her concerns and fears boiled over in a verbal affront to his stupidity.

"And sometimes they don't come back at all!" she snapped. "Men. You just don't get it."

He looked up momentarily with a puzzled expression but quickly returned his gaze to the son before him.

Elizabeth was upset with his attitude. But there was something that bothered her more. The ease of the birth. That disturbed her deeply. She secretly wished there had been some problems. Any problems. Problems were expected. The lack of them wasn't normal. God's Word said that a woman's sorrow would be multiplied in childbirth. It was evident this birth came from another hand.

"The Good Book says, because of Eve's sin, women will suffer in childbirth," Elizabeth said out loud. "When are you men going to suffer for your sins?"

18

True enough, Elizabeth had seen easy births. She'd seen none as easy as this. True, each birth was different; each had its own complications. But this was the first one she'd ever seen where there were NO problems.

That, combined with the birth coming during the depth of the eclipse, was a bad omen. This child was marked by the hell-wolf of darkness. Elizabeth feared what evil this life would bring to the valley.

Earlier, when the newborn had slipped into her hands and she'd started cleaning him off, she noticed something amiss. The last two toes on his left foot were grown together. Cloven hooves. A sure mark of Satan. She finished cleaning him off, rubbing him all over with the garlic. Then she wrapped it in a flannel blanket.

For a brief moment, she considered smothering the baby. Priscilla was at the fire, her back turned. Sarah couldn't see what was taking place, and she probably wouldn't remember it anyway. The men were still outside. She could just hold her hand over its little nose and mouth and it would be over quickly. But she hesitated and the opportunity was lost.

Turning back to the bed, she found Hans and Benjamin standing in the cabin door. All eyes were now on her as she placed the child on his mother's breast. The opportunity was gone.

"Come see your new son," Sarah called softly to her husband.

Elizabeth reluctantly backed away.

As Sarah showed their son to her husband, the world marched again toward light. Benjamin and Sarah looked at the baby and then at each other. A smile passed between them. Probably the first Sarah had gotten from him in a long time.

"It's like a sign, isn't it?" Sarah bubbled. "Two sunrises in the same day."

Benjamin looked at her with a quizzical expression.

"The first sunrise appeared this morning, just as it should have," she said. "Now, with the light rising once again, this is a second sunrise."

"I guess you could look at it that way," Benjamin said.

"And our baby brought the second one," she sighed. "That must mean something good!"

Elizabeth knew that the child had not come with the warming light. He had slipped from the womb during the cold-hearted center of the darkness. This was not a blessed event. It was a curse. Of that much, she was certain.

"Sarah, you and Ben got a name picked out?" Elizabeth did her best to sound cheery.

"We've thought about a few. But nothing definite."

Like a thousand mothers before her, Sarah lovingly traced her finger down her son's cheek.

"I'm partial to Loel," Benjamin said. "After my pa."

"I've given it some thought too," Elizabeth said. "Coming over in the wagon, I realized he might come with the eclipse."

"Was that what that was?" Priscilla asked brushing at her dress. "I've heard of them, but never seen one."

"That's what it was," Hans said.

"Yes," Elizabeth continued. "And I've got a name I'd like to offer."

"What's that?" Sarah asked. "What name do you suggest?"

"Caleb."

"A good, strong name for a boy," Benjamin Ranklin scratched his hairy chin.

"But why that name over another?"

"It's Biblical."

Elizabeth had given the idea a lot of thought. Now she wanted to convince the Ranklin's that it would be a good choice.

"Caleb and Joseph were with Moses," she said, "when the tribe of Israel was wandering in the wilderness."

"That's true," said Sarah. "I've read that."

"They're the only two who believed in God's promise. Because of that, God said Caleb's seed would possess the Promised Land."

Elizabeth waited for the idea to gain some hold in the new parent's minds. While Benjamin might not know much about scripture, Elizabeth hoped Sarah might set some store in it. She quickly added, "Caleb and Joseph were the only two who made it to the Promised Land."

From the looks on Benjamin and Sarah's faces, Elizabeth knew her words were beginning to carry some weight.

"Since, like you say," Elizabeth talked fast, "he was born as the light was coming back. Maybe this means that his seed will transform this dark and wild land into a new Promised Land."

130

As weak as it was, Elizabeth's suggestion couldn't have fallen on more receptive ears. Sarah was intrigued by the idea of her son having a Biblical name. Benjamin knew his son was special and should carry a special name.

"I like the name Caleb," Sarah looked up at her husband.

"Then Caleb it is!" Benjamin stuck out his chest.

"Caleb Loel Ranklin," he said. "It's a sign. He's going to help me possess my Promised Land. We're going to regain all of the land that was stolen from me."

"Good," Elizabeth said. "Then that's settled. Now you men get out of here. We women have still got some things that need tending to."

By late evening, everything was in order. Elizabeth decided it was time they left. She didn't want to linger at the dark cabin any longer. The devil was in his power. He had been exposed today, and tonight would be a new moon. She didn't want to ride home in total darkness.

"We'll leave you to get acquainted with your new baby." Elizabeth hoped her haste wouldn't be apparent.

"Priscilla here can take care of you just fine. She's got enough experience to know how to take care of you both. If you need me for anything, I'm within hollering distance."

Hans and Elizabeth said their good-byes and were soon on their way home. They were well up Owen's Creek before Hans broke the silence.

"Where'd you come up with the name Caleb?" Hans cut a sideways frown at his wife. "You know as well as I do, that child is not blessed from God."

"Yes, I know. But they don't know that," Elizabeth said. "If I told them the real reason for the name, they would have refused it."

"Just what was your reason?" Hans couldn't wait to hear this one. "I never once believed all that bull about the Promised Land. Why Caleb?"

"In Hebrew, Caleb means dog," Elizabeth said. "When I first saw him, my heart felt like it had been dunked in Little Piney during the depth of winter."

"I felt the cold too," Hans said.

"That baby's the spawn of the devil. Did you see those cloven feet?" Elizabeth asked. "He's the devil-wolf that ate the sun. The devil's dog himself...Caleb."

"It would have been better if that one had been stillborn," Hans said.

"He nearly was."

Elizabeth admitted she had nearly suffocated him before Hans and Benjamin entered the room. "I just couldn't do it," she said. "But mark my words, there's evil in that child. Bad things will come to this valley."

They rode on, both lost in their own thoughts. It would be years before Hans and Elizabeth would have occasion to discuss Caleb's destiny again. But, on this day, in the gathering gloom of nightfall, they both knew that evil would come. Yes, it would come. They just didn't know what it would be or when to expect it.

But time has a way of making you put things out of your mind. It was no different with Caleb's birth. It too, slipped slowly into the fog of daily life. More children were born into the valley. First one family, then another, needed Elizabeth's granny woman skills.

Even the O'Brien's had more children. In 1835 they had another son. They named him Timothy. And in 1836 they had a daughter. The valley was slowly filling up with families and youngsters. Most of the valley residents welcomed the growth. Some did not.

19

The week following Caleb's birth, Elizabeth decided to call on her neighbor. Hans had been by the Ranklin cabin but had not seen Benjamin around lately. Elizabeth feared Sarah had been left alone with her new baby.

"Ben's probably out hunting or some such," he told Elizabeth.

"Sarah don't need to be taking care of a new baby all by herself," Elizabeth said. "Don't that man know she might need help? Or does he even care?"

"I'm pretty sure he ain't been around the last couple of days," Hans said. "Maybe Priscilla is checking in on her."

Well, I better get over there and check on her myself," Elizabeth said. "If you'll hitch up that old mule, I'll fix something to take over there."

Elizabeth already had some chicken with broth simmering on the fire. While Hans hitched up the wagon, she ladled some up in a cast iron pot and packed it in a basket. Soon she was making her way over the gravel trail between Owen's Creek and the Ranklin cabin on Devil's Fork. Every new mother could use a little extra help.

Sarah was standing in the open doorway of the cabin with a broom in her hand when the wagon rattled up into the yard.

"Get down and come in," she seemed glad to have company.

"Wanted to check on you and Caleb," Elizabeth said. "Brought you a little something."

Elizabeth headed the wagon toward a gum sapling where she could tie the mule. She didn't want him wandering off with the wagon while she was visiting. Sarah leaned the broom against the door jam and walked out to meet Elizabeth.

Elizabeth handed down the pot of broth and climbed down from the wagon. After securing the mule, they headed inside the cabin, both with big smiles on their faces.

"How's Caleb?" Elizabeth asked.

"He's doing just fine," Sarah chirped. "He's sleeping right now. Been wearing me thin though, cries all night and sleeps all day. Think he's got his days and nights mixed up."

"They sometimes do that," Elizabeth said and sympathetically patted Sarah on the back.

Once inside, Sarah motioned for Elizabeth to sit at the roughhewn table. She hung the pot from a metal hook and swung it over coals still hot from the morning's fire.

"That should heat up nicely," Sarah said. "Sure smells good."

"A meal somebody else fixed always smells good," Elizabeth smiled. "Whether it really is or not."

"I'm sure it will be fine."

After checking on the baby sleeping peacefully on the bed, Elizabeth sat down at the table. Sarah joined her and the two women talked like old friends catching up on bits of gossip.

"If you don't mind me asking," Elizabeth said. "I'm curious. I don't think I've ever been told how you and Benjamin met."

"As you already know," Sarah began. "Ben came out here when this was wild country. Right after the government bought it. They called it the Louisiana Purchase back then. He was a trapper and Indian trader."

Over the next couple of hours, Sarah told of her husband exploring, trapping, and trading with the Indians all along the Arkansas River. He had been good at what he did and had amassed a nice sum of money. There was some kind of falling out with his employers, the St. Louis Fur Company, and he decided to move back home to Tennessee. That's where they'd met.

"I was married before," Sarah said. "To a wonderful man. We were together for seven years. But we never had children." Sarah's eyes took on a sad look, remembering some unpleasant memory.

"One day," she began. "He was castrating young bulls, and one of 'em stepped on his foot. I wrapped the wound with a coal oil rag, but gangrene set in."

"Didn't he see a doctor," Elizabeth said. "Surely they could have done something."

"We had a doctor look at him," Sarah said. "He wanted to cut the foot off."

"Did that help?"

"It might have. If he'd let the doc do it. But first, he refused to let him have the foot. As the rot progressed, he refused to let him have the leg. Said he wouldn't be no cripple. Hobbling around on a crutch."

"I've seen some gangrene," Elizabeth said. "It is a tough way to go."

"It was an agonizing illness," Sarah said. "Stunk real bad too. When he finally passed, he left me with a mortgage and no way to pay it."

"What did you do?"

"I lost everything we'd built," she said. "Moved in with some friends from church. They's nice enough, but every day I felt like a burden on the family. That's when I was introduced to Benjamin Ranklin."

"And you two fell in love."

"Well," Sarah began. "Not exactly. Ben and Jacob was getting ready to move back here. To this valley Ben'd discovered while trading with the Indians. Made it sound like paradise. Told me he'd traded for an old Spanish Land Grant and that he owned the entire valley. He was looking for a wife to share it all."

"Surely there was some affection there," Elizabeth said. "To just pull up stakes and head way out here."

"I'd been married to a younger man," Sarah said. "And it was a struggle from the start. When he died, I was in worse circumstances than before we'd married. Now, here was another man, asking for my hand in marriage. He was much older than me, but he already had a life made. He owned an entire valley. I was sure we could make it work."

"And so far, you have."

"You know the saying," she laughed. "It's better to be an old man's sweetheart, than a young man's slave."

"Yes," Elizabeth agreed, "I've heard that."

"We weren't in love," Sarah admitted. "He wanted a wife and I needed a husband. It was simply a marriage of convenience."

"But everything's good. Right?"

"Don't repeat this to a soul," she made Elizabeth promise. "But it's been rough at times."

"Everybody has rough patches," Elizabeth said.

"That's true," Sarah said. "And he don't beat me near like Jacob beats Priscilla."

Elizabeth was suddenly at a loss for words. She had suspicions that Jacob was a bully to his wife. But she hadn't dreamed that Benjamin practiced the same abuse.

Before she could form a response, Sarah continued. "Ever since I became pregnant with Caleb," Sarah said. "Things have been nicer."

"Don't you get lonely?" Elizabeth asked. "With him gone all the time."

"I used to," she responded. "But now I've got my son. Nothing else matters."

"Well, you need to take care of that boy," Elizabeth said. "Read the Good Book to him every day. He's going to need a lot of help."

"What makes you say that?"

Elizabeth couldn't come right out and tell Sarah that her son was the Devil's own. Instead, she came up with a plausible reply. "All boys need direction." She tried to change the subject.

"I'd best get back home," she said. "I left Hans by himself and there's no telling what kind of trouble he's found by now."

"I hope you come visit again soon," Sarah said. "I sure could use some adult company from time to time."

"I'll be back," Elizabeth said. "And remember, you're welcome at our place anytime."

"I appreciate that," Sarah said.

From the expression on her face, Elizabeth knew Sarah really meant what she said. It would be lonely with nothing but a child to talk with. And this child couldn't even talk back yet. Maybe that was a good thing though.

With that, Elizabeth excused herself and headed back up Devil's Fork and toward home. At her core, Sarah was a good woman. Even if she was saddled with a questionable husband. Hopefully, she would be able to set Caleb's feet on the straight path.

20

"Hello the house," a voice called out.

Helen opened the kitchen door tentatively. Benjamin Ranklin sat atop an appaloosa stud, a rifle resting across the pommel of his saddle. She had recognized the voice immediately. She slid her hand across her own musket, propped against the doorpost, reassured by its presence.

"Morning Mr. Ranklin," Helen said. "What brings you to *our* hollow?" Helen couldn't help but emphasize the ownership placed in the word our. Benjamin's fur-clad presence and his dead eyes unnerved her, but she wasn't going to let him know that. Not if she could help it.

"Thought I'd drop by for a friendly visit." A sickening grin pulled at the corners of his mouth. "Irish around?"

"He might be down by the mill," Helen lied. "Should be back soon."

"That's a little fib now, ain't it?"

The mountain man put his weight on the stirrups, shifting forward in the saddle. The leather creaked loudly under his weight.

"I seen him and that boy," he said. "They left in the wagon around daylight. From the looks of things, he's planning of being gone for a day or two."

"That's right," Helen tried to recover. "They were headed over to the Göbel's to pick up some things. They'll be back shortly."

"I think he's gone to Spadra or Lewisburg." Ranklin swung down from the appaloosa, his moccasined feet touching lightly in the grass just off the porch.

"Gone off and left a sweet thing like you all alone for a few days."

He wiped a buckskin sleeve against his whiskered mouth. Reaching up, he swept his coyote skin cap from his head and bowed slightly at the waist, keeping his black eyes on Helen as he did so.

"Not a smart thing to do with all these strangers moving into the valley here lately," he said. "Some of 'em ain't from polite society. Wouldn't know how to treat a fine lady like yourself."

"You claiming yourself respectable?" Helen challenged.

"Now Mrs. O'Brien," again with the grin. "May I call you Helen?" He continued without waiting for a response. "That's not a neighborly thing to say to a man."

With the quickness of a cat, he stepped onto the porch and swept into the kitchen before Helen knew what he was doing. She reached for the musket but was too late. As she started to pick it up, his meaty paw was already taking it from her.

"See you got this primed and ready," he observed. "That's good. Never can be too careful. Don't know who might slip up on a body."

As he shoved his way past her, she nearly stumbled as she back away. He looked around the large kitchen taking in all the details that were missing from his own dirt floor cabin. The cast-iron stove held a pot of coffee, its aroma filling the room.

"Irish has built you a nice place here," he said. "Too bad you have to share it with a thief."

"You need to leave, Mr. Ranklin!"

"Now that ain't no way to be," he said. "Ain't you going to offer a weary traveler a cup of coffee?"

He sat down at the big oak table in one of the straight-backed chairs. Its legs protested to the sudden weight, making a squeaking sound as he shifted around, making himself comfortable.

"One cup of coffee and then you leave," she said with as much strength as she could muster.

Helen wanted him to leave, but was afraid to make him mad. If she let him have a cup of coffee and say his piece, maybe he would leave without causing any real trouble.

"See now," he said. "It don't hurt none to be nice."

Helen walked over to the cupboard and got out one coffee cup. Picking up the coffee pot from the stovetop, she brought them both to the table. She placed the cup in front of him, careful to keep the table between them. Her hands were trembling slightly, and she sloshed some on the table.

"Careful there," he said.

"Drink your coffee and leave."

"We should have some pleasant conversation to go with this fine coffee. How have you been lately, Helen?"

"I've been just fine, thank you," Helen said through clenched teeth.

"Fine you are!" He leaned back in the chair. "Finer'n frog hair split four ways, I'd say."

"You can keep your opinions to yourself," her green eyes narrowed.

"Say, ain't you got another youngster around," he asked.

"Yes, I have another son." Helen suddenly feared for a life other than her own.

"He's still asleep in the other room."

"That's right."

Ranklin raised the coffee cup to his lips and blew slightly. Before taking a sip, he said, "You enjoy making babies, don't you?" He waited for his words to take effect. "How'd you like to make one with a real man?"

"Mr. Ranklin," Helen stamped her foot, "I will not be talked to this way."

"Irish ain't much of a man." His piggish, black eyes showed no emotion. "I'm sure he has trouble satisfying the passions of a vibrant woman like yourself." A grin played at the corners of his mouth. "Why don't you just come over here and sit in a real man's lap?"

"That sir is quite enough!"

Helen fought to keep the fear from showing in her voice. She was certain it showed in her eyes. "What would your wife Sarah say to this?"

"Who cares what she thinks?" He scooted his chair away from the table, making a rasping, scraping sound. "Right now, I'm just asking," he said. "I could be taking. Just like your husband took what was mine."

"You can keep your nasty asking to yourself," Helen said. "And if you go to taking, Patrick will kill you," her eyes flashed. "If he don't—I will."

"Getting a little hot, aren't you?" he snickered.

"How about I pour this coffee in your lap?" Her green eyes narrowed to slits. "Then we'll see what's hot."

"Pull back on the reins a mite, Mrs. O'Brien."

"I think it's high time you left!" her jaws tightened.

"Okay. I'll leave...for now."

He rose and moved toward the door, hesitated before going out into the yard. He looked over his shoulder. "But you might best convince your husband he needs to get out of my hollow, else I'll be back. And next time the conversation might not be so polite."

"The next time you ride up into this yard," Helen said. "You'll be met with buckshot."

Ranklin swung up into the saddle and galloped out of the yard laughing. Helen walked over to the table and collapsed in a chair. With her head resting on her arms, she cried.

What was she to do? If she said nothing, he might come back. If she told her husband everything that had transpired, his temper would demand he go after Ranklin. That might get her husband killed. Ranklin hadn't done anything, other than threaten. What should she do?

21

The bond between the O'Brien's and Göbel's grew with every shared event and each faced the challenge. Each knew that when push came to shove, they had a dependable friend. They became an extended family. One held together by trust and love.

When demand grew heavy at the sawmill, Hans filled in like he was part owner. Doing every job from off-loading slabs to figuring how many board feet could be cut from a log. He became very good at the latter. Patrick, on the other hand, along with all the O'Brien's, helped pick and press Hans' grapes in season. Of course, Patrick helped taste the results of the fermentation process, just so he could give a fair appraisal of the product.

Elizabeth and Hans still had no children of their own. But as the O'Brien family grew, in reality, so did theirs. Connell and Killian were both growing like milkweed and felt as comfortable at one home as the other.

This extended family grew by another boy, Timothy O'Brien, in 1835. And on February 2, 1836, the family expanded once again by the addition of a girl.

"Patrick," Helen said, "I think it's time to fetch Elizabeth."

"Is the baby coming?" Fear was evident in Patrick's voice.

"Take it easy," Helen smiled. "My water hasn't broken. Nothing like that. I just feel it'll be soon."

"I'll get her. She said not to wait until the last minute. You and the boys will be all right until I get back."

Elizabeth Göbel had given him strict orders. She wanted to be notified early. "Patrick O'Brien, don't you dare wait until the last minute," she'd demanded. "Come get me as soon as she starts feeling anything out of the ordinary. I've got godchildren I'm responsible for."

Patrick saddled the mare in the cool February morning air and headed for the Göbel homestead. Taking the trail out of Cliffy Hollow, he rode down the valley and splashed across the Little Piney just above the spot where Devil's Fork entered it. From there he turned up Devil's Fork, riding past the Ranklin places and up toward Owens Creek.

As he was passing the Ranklin's cabin, something struck the mare just behind the saddle, causing her to bolt. It took a few jumps before Patrick got her back under control. If he'd been less of a horseman, the start would have unseated him.

Glancing over his shoulder he saw Benjamin Ranklin standing in the edge of the trees on the hillside. He had a rock in his right hand, tossing it up and catching it. It was plain what had happened.

Patrick considered stopping long enough to teach him a lesson. But today he didn't have time to play games. With a glare in Ranklin's direction, he urged the mare on her way. Benjamin's laughter nettled his ears until it was lost in the distance.

The Göbel's and Patrick were soon on their way back down the trail toward Little Piney, the Göbel's in their wagon and Patrick riding alongside. When they reached the Ranklin's run-down cabin, Benjamin was still standing beside the trail, waiting. Ignoring Patrick, he directed his question to Elizabeth.

"Where you off to?" he demanded. "In case Sarah and the boy need your services."

"Helen O'Brien is about to give birth," Elizabeth replied. "Is there some reason you think you might need me?"

"Naw," Ben scratched at his beard then cut smoldering eyes in Patrick's direction. "Another Irish coming into this valley?" he snarled. "Too many of you O'Brien's around already."

"I might say the same for Ranklin's," Patrick shot back.

"There ain't no time for such trash talk," Elizabeth glared at both men. "There's more important things in this world than two grown men acting like schoolboys fighting over chalk."

"One of these days, Irish," Benjamin warned. "I'll come claim my land."

"Come claim your six feet of it," Patrick flashed back, "any time you want."

"Get up there mule," Hans called out, slapping the reins on the gray mule's rump. The wagon lurched forward, jerking the spring seat into motion along with the wagon.

"We're wasting time," he said. "Nothing's getting settled this way."

As the Gobel's and Patrick rode away, Benjamin called out, "Irish, my son will want his birthright."

"And my children will keep theirs," Patrick shouted without turning around.

Once back home in Cliffy Hollow, Patrick checked on Helen and the boys. Everything seemed to be in good shape, so he left Helen in Elizabeth's capable hands and went down to the mill with Hans.

Since the mill was not working, there was no need for the water wheel to be turning. Patrick had shut the gate on the millrace. Water filled the trough and splashed over, back into the creek.

"Got another order for lumber," he said. "Might need your help next week. After the baby gets here."

"I'll be ready," Hans said.

"Elizabeth said the baby might come tonight, day after tomorrow at the latest."

"Then we'll need something to celebrate with."

Patrick reached over into the cool water of the millrace and pulled out a brown jug. He swirled it in a circular motion, its contents splashing noisily.

"This soldier's nearly gone," he smiled.

"If the baby's not here by tonight, I'll head back home," Hans said. "But Elizabeth will spend the next few days over here. When I return captain, I'll bring replacements."

"Good." Patrick eased the jug back into the cool water. "Now what's going on with Ranklin?"

"Same as always," Hans said. "He thinks you stole Cliffy Hollow and he ain't gonna give up on getting it back."

"Well, he'll just have to," Patrick said. "I didn't steal it, and I durn sure ain't leaving."

"When I rode by his place the other day," Hans said, "he said he'd be bringing you down a peg or two."

"Tis just talk. Every terrier is bold in the doorway of its own home," Patrick observed. "And if it's a fight he wants. I'll oblige him. I can give as good as I get."

Their discussion was cut short by the arrival of Connell.

"Papa," Connell, his words short and quick. "You're wanted at the house right away."

Patrick ran back up to the house, Connell and Hans following close behind. Bursting into the house, he stomped upstairs, startling Killian and Timothy, who began to whimper.

"Is it time?" Patrick asked his breath coming in short gasps.

"You men," Elizabeth placed both hands on her hips. "Try to calm down some. I just wanted you to know her water broke. It won't be long."

"What do you need me to do?"

"You can take them two older boys downstairs. I'll try to settle the baby down. Now that you've scared him nearly out of his wits." Elizabeth turned and smiled at Helen. "Now that your water broke," she said, "your contractions will start getting pretty regular now."

Helen smiled, then grimaced as another contraction gripped her. "I expect the new baby will be here shortly."

"Shortly?" Patrick's face was a mixture of pure happiness and fear.

"Think you might find something to feed them two boys?" Elizabeth said. "You might not be hungry, but I suspect them boys are."

Patrick hustled the two older boys back down the stairs. He was too nervous to think about eating, but Elizabeth was right about the boys. Patrick went out to the smokehouse and trimmed some thin strips off a ham. Back in the kitchen, he placed it in a skillet on the stove and stoked up the fire. Next, he peeled and cut up potatoes which he added to a second cast-iron skillet. Soon the kitchen was full of the smells of potatoes frying and the sound of sizzling meat.

It was after dark when Patrick took the boys upstairs to the other bedroom. Hans curled up on the floor of the downstairs family room.

Patrick climbed into bed with his older sons and soon had them asleep. The baby boy was sleeping in the room where his mother was about to have his newest sibling. Sometime around midnight, Patrick, too, succumbed to the arms of Morpheus. But his dreams were fitful.

The next morning, he overslept. The sun washed the upper reaches of the cedar tree just off the front porch of the cabin when he was startled by the cries of a newborn.

With the coming of a new day, on February 2, 1836, under the sign of a full moon, Josephine Etaine O'Brien came screaming into Patrick's world.

Leaping out of bed, he quickly crossed the hall into his wife's bedroom. Elizabeth was holding a bundle of pink sunshine, and both she and Helen were beaming.

"How's Helen?" were his first words.

"Momma's fine," Elizabeth said.

"And the baby?" he asked.

"Your daughter is fine too," Elizabeth said.

"Daughter?"

Patrick didn't stand a chance. He was instantly captivated by the sight of his seventh child. A daughter. One glance at the wrinkled face, the little fingers clenched into a tiny fist, and he was lost. As the sun rose in the east, Josephine became the new light of her father's life.

"May I hold her?" he asked.

Elizabeth tucked her tighter into the flannel blanket and gently offered her to Patrick. Taking her gently into his hands, he held her close to his chest. Josephine was going to be the spitting image of her mother. He couldn't believe the blessing he had received. Although he'd lost three boys to the deplorable conditions in the slums of New York, things had turned around. He had a loving wife, three strapping sons, and now a beautiful daughter.

The love filling his heart made him lightheaded. Looking into Josephine's emerald eyes, he quoted an Irish poem:

> "May the leprechauns be near you,
> To spread luck along your way.
> And may all the Irish angels,
> Smile upon you this day."

A gas bubble made her turn her mouth into a crooked little smile. But Patrick knew it was angels, kissing her on the cheek. As Helen had captured his heart years earlier, Josephine made the surrender complete. His heart would never again belong to him.

Josephine weighed a little over six pounds, with a head of curly, red hair. Instead of the blue eyes that most babies have at birth, Josephine's eyes were a deep, emerald green. They would remain that brilliant, captivating green throughout her life. The combination of her engaging, green eyes and her curly, auburn hair ensured she would draw attention.

Patrick reluctantly returned her to her mother. As he laid her in Helen's arms, he gave both mother and daughter a kiss on the forehead. Helen snuggled her daughter close, smiled at Patrick, then she too kissed Josephine's forehead.

"Elizabeth," Helen said. "You and Hans need children of your own." Helen wanted her best friend to be as happy as she was right now. "When are ya'll gonna do something about that?"

"Hush now! You're talking out of your head." Elizabeth patted Helen's hand. "You know Hans' only got time for his grapes. Anyway, don't I have just the grandest godsons of my own to spoil, whenever I want?"

Elizabeth took a deep breath that expressed her own pride and happiness. "And now," she said, "such a goddaughter!"

"She is beautiful." Helen pulled the cover from around Josephine's face. Even if it was her daughter, she had never seen a more beautiful child.

"That's because she's the spitting image of her ma," Elizabeth reached out for Josephine. "Now, hand her over. Time for me to start spoiling. And it's time for you to get some rest!"

Elizabeth took the baby and sat down in a rocker beside Helen's bed. As she rocked, she sang a German lullaby. Josephine went immediately to sleep.

Patrick stood at the door to the room, his arms folded on his chest. Lost in the moment, his eyes filled with tears. The luckiest man in the world.

"Now, you git too," Elizabeth said in mock scorn. "Men folk do blessed little to get them here, then they wanna puff up and strut, like they done something great."

"Thank you, Elizabeth."

She waved her hand at Patrick as if sweeping him out of the room. "Guess you can go brag about it now. Go tell Hans what a man you are. These two need their rest."

"Isn't there anything I can do?"

"You've done quite enough. Now be gone with you."

As an afterthought, she added. "Bring the boys up to see their sister after breakfast. Now skedaddle!"

22

During the first year the O'Brien's built their home, Patrick stumbled across a small family living in a hunting camp in the upper reaches of Cliffy Hollow. Black Fox was a Cherokee sub-chief who had refused to move his family west during the Indian removal. Educated at Dwight Mission, with ancestors buried in the surrounding mountains, his roots in the area were strong.

Pride in ancestry was something Patrick understood. He and Black Fox found an immediate common ground. Instead of running the Cherokee off his land, like others had been doing, he made it clear that Black Fox's family were welcome to stay where they were.

Over time, the trust grew even stronger. Patrick furnished Black Fox with lumber to build a regular home, one like he'd grown up in before the Indian Removal. The families visited often, each being welcome at the other's home fire. At every opportunity, the O'Brien children pestered Black Fox to teach them woodcraft. Especially Connell.

Black Fox taught the children to respect wildlife and all that the Great Spirit had provided. He taught them never to kill for amusement, only for food. And when a quail or squirrel gave their life to sustain yours, you should thank them for that life they were giving.

They were taught how to read signs left by their fellow-creatures. How bits of pinecones scattered under a tree told where the fox squirrel had eaten its fill of pine seeds. How the round pellets on top of a log told where a rabbit had gotten up off the ground to relieve itself. How the tracks of the bobcat found in the sandy trail told of his search for the rabbit. And that the hand-like print of a raccoon on a muddy creek bank showed where it had fished for crawfish and washed his meal.

He taught them how to find dry tinder to start a fire after a rain. Which plants could be used for food, and which served as medicine. Eventually, as the children grew, he gave the family Cherokee names. Names with meaning that fit something about them or their personality.

He called Patrick *Outacity*, or man-killer, after a Cherokee chief. For Patrick was the chief of the O'Brien clan. He would do whatever was necessary to protect his family. Helen he called *Ahyoka* the bringer of happiness. Connell he called *Woha'li*, or eagle, because of his superior eyesight and noble carriage. Killian he called *Gitli-dihi'*, or killer of dogs, because of an incident that happened involving a rabid cur dog. Timothy became *Degataga* which translated to standing together. Jospehine he named *Da nagasta*, or eager warrior because she was as ready for a fight as any brave.

Black Fox was unselfish with his time when it came to the O'Brien children. He taught them many things, but he could only teach that which they were ready to learn. Patrick too encouraged the children's curiosity, but neither man coddled them.

In the fall of 1840, Connell was nine years old. Lean and tall for his age, a ball of energy in constant motion.

Always trying something new. Whether learning things about timber from his father or investigating the ways of the wild with Black Fox, his mind craved to know the why's about things. His curiosity sometimes got him into trouble.

"Hard learned lessons are the best-learned lessons," Patrick was telling Connell. He was dobbing wet tobacco on a few hornet stings at the time. A new lesson Connell had just been taught.

"I guess you'll not be throwing rocks at a hornet nest again."

"No, sir."

Connell had hollered when the hornet first popped him, but he hadn't cried. Patrick knew the angry, red whelps hurt something terrible, but Connell wasn't about to show signs of being weak.

"But that durn nest is right beside the apple orchard," he said. "And them hornets are everywhere."

"You just leave it alone," Patrick smiled.

"I bet every spoiled apple has a hun'nerd bees on it."

"You heard me."

Patrick's voice took that stern edge he hoped would sink into his children's head. "I said leave that hornet nest alone."

"Yes, sir."

Patrick wrapped a cloth around Connell's leg to keep the tobacco in place.

"But I don't understand how them hornets spotted me so quick." Connell fidgeted, not able to sit still. The sting from the hornet felt as if it were on fire. "As soon as I threw the rock, I ducked behind a tree."

"They still found you though, didn't they?"

Patrick could see the wheels working in his son's mind. This was how he would learn, by making mistakes and paying the price. Maybe someday the youngster would learn by watching others make the mistakes. Heaven knew he had made enough mistakes of his own.

"Is it true," Connell asked, "what Mr. MacGregor said?"

"What did old man MacGregor say?"

"He said them hornets can follow the arch of something thrown—right back to you?"

"No, that's not true," Patrick chuckled. "Although some think it."

"How'd they find me so quick then?"

"You ever notice hornets crawling around the hole at the bottom of the nest?"

"Yes."

"They're always there," Patrick said. "Like soldiers on picket duty. Their job is to protect their own. If some little boy comes along with a pocket full of rocks and nothing better to do, they're ready. Something shakes the nest, like an inquisitive possum or your well-flung rock; they fly out in every direction to find the cause. In this case, you. They give the alarm, and the rest come a swarming. You might want to remember that, it could come in handy someday."

That lesson and a hundred others were not wasted on Connell. He seemed to soak up every adventure and always looked for more. Such was the case later when the first frost tinged the early morning.

"Papa," he asked, "would you help me build a rabbit trap?"

"Why you want to do that?" Patrick never knew what to expect from his oldest. "You think you're big enough to handle a big buck rabbit?"

"Yes, sir."

Connell talked fast. His Papa was listening and he didn't want to squander the opportunity for a new adventure.

"I bet I could catch a nice fat rabbit along the fence line. If'n I did, he sure would eat good."

"A fat hare would be nice."

Connell could see his Papa starting to give in. "You might even catch a fat possum," Patrick teased. "Think you could make a possum sull?"

"I ain't scared of no possum!" Connell squinted his eyes and pouted his lips. "I know how to knock one out with a stick."

"No, you ain't scared of much." Patrick couldn't help but laugh. "I'll give you that. But sometimes you ought to be."

Patrick thought about the idea. Fresh rabbit sure would be tasty, and it was cold enough to make the meat good. A small trap line would teach Connell some good lessons, like being responsible and how to think ahead and plan.

"You know you'll have to set the traps every evening," he said. "And run them first thing the next morning?" Patrick wanted Connell to understand that laziness would not be tolerated. Nor would he abide the mistreatment of an animal. Death was a necessary part of living. To eat, one must kill. But unnecessary cruelty to another living creature had no place in the O'Brien family.

"I promise I'll run them every day."

"Okay. Fetch a saw." Patrick headed toward the barn. "I'll get the mule. I know where there are some hollow gum trees down in the flat."

Connell returned with the saw before Patrick had the halter on the mule. Together, they headed out of the barnyard, past the house and toward the creek.

As they passed the house, Patrick called out to the other boys. "Killian, you and Timothy come on."

"Where we going, Papa?" Killian asked.

"Just you come on here." Patrick reached down, picked Timothy up and swung him up on the back of the old mule. "You boys are going to learn something."

"Can I ride too?" Killian asked.

Patrick grabbed him under his arms and in one motion swung him high overhead, plopping him down behind his younger brother. "You boys hang on tight."

Helen came to the door of the cabin. Four-year-old Josephine at her side, one hand clinging to her mother's apron; the other thumb stuck in her mouth.

"Where are my menfolk off to?" Helen called after them.

"We're gone foraging," Connell sang out.

"Going down by the creek," Patrick added. "Be back shortly."

Helen watched after them as they headed down toward Cliffy Creek. Passing by an old cedar tree, they were momentarily framed against its green backdrop. Patrick had halted the mule and was pointing at a flock of passenger pigeons winging their way over the far field. It was a small flock, probably no more than a couple hundred birds. Helen could imagine Patrick explaining to the boys that the birds were on their way to the pin oak flats to fatten up on acorns.

She knew the image would remain frozen in her memory forever. Her husband leading the mule, his head not much taller than the mule's withers; her five and seven-year-old sons perched bravely on the mule's back, and her nine-year-old walking proudly beside his father. The men in her life, off on an adventure.

Patrick and the boys were soon in the woods near the creek. He had no problem finding the hollow gum trees he had seen earlier.

"Here we go Connell," Patrick said. "Just what we need to make them rabbit traps."

Taking the younger boys down from the mule, he tied the mule's halter to a large huckleberry bush. The mule wasted no time sticking his muzzle into the bush and began chewing at the leaves.

"You boys keep an eye out for copperheads," Patrick cautioned. "They blend in good in the leaves. Been cool enough they should be denned up by now, but it pays to be careful. Me and Connell have got some sawing to do."

"Which gum log we going to use Papa?" Connell asked.

"Well, let's see," Patrick rubbed at his chin. "We'll need one with a hollow heart, but solid on the outside. The hollow needs to be big enough for a rabbit to get inside, but not too big. We don't want him turning around once he gets in. And, we don't want a bigger animal getting trapped."

Patrick reached out and tousled Connell's hair. "Wouldn't want to find a wildcat in there would you?"

Connell looked as if he was about to claim he wasn't scared of no wildcat. He must have thought better of it. Instead, he grinned and asked, "How long they need to be?"

"About three feet."

"How many we gonna make?" Connell asked.

"Might as well make three while we're at it," Patrick replied. "Improve our chances that way."

"Hey Papa," Killian shouted. "Look what we found."

Killian and Timothy were wading up to their knees in the quiet stream. They were turning over rocks to see what would scoot out from underneath. Something had caught their attention. Patrick walked over to the creek bank to inspect their find.

"Let me see what you've got there."

"Ain't no snake," said Killian. "It's got legs."

"By golly, it has," Patrick smiled. "Boys you've got yourself a salamander."

"Bug," said Timothy.

"No, son. It ain't a bug," Patrick smiled. "More like a water-bound lizard."

"Can we eat it?" asked Killian.

"I don't think salamanders would taste good," Patrick laughed. "Anyway, it'd take quite a few to make a mess."

Connell momentarily drew Patrick's attention away from the explorers. "There's a good log over here that might work, Papa."

"All right," Patrick said. "Fetch the saw."

Connell went running to get the saw that was tied on the mule. In a few seconds, he was back.

"We'll cut 'em to length here," Patrick explained. "Then we'll take 'em up to the sawmill to drill the hole for the trip stick.

And we'll build the trap door on one end and block off the other." Connell wanted Patrick to know he knew what he was doing. "Right Papa?"

"That's right, son."

"What can I use for bait?"

"Cut-up apples should do just fine."

Connell and Patrick got to work. In no time they were nearly through. It was about that time that Killian and Timothy started a gumball fight.

23

The seven years since the O'Brien's came to the Little Piney valley, had drifted by like the seven years of plenty. There was land to work, timber to cut, and homes to build. Children were growing and Patrick's sawmill was becoming a going enterprise.

During that time Arkansas became a state, there had been a siege at a little adobe Mission down in Mexico called the Alamo, and President Van Buren took office. Back East, a financial panic followed Van Buren's election. People lost everything due to land speculation and crop failures. Another westward migration began.

The population of the newly formed 25th state doubled and doubled again. Every month, more and more people poured into Little Piney Valley. They wanted lumber for houses and barns and the O'Brien sawmill was a hive of activity from sunup to sunset. Things were popping.

It was a common occurrence for wagons and individual horsemen to ride up to the mill throughout the day. It was no surprise that no one noticed the fur-clad mountain man on the appaloosa until he was sitting right outside the mill door.

Conversations ceased as people recognized the rider. Slowly, work came to a halt and the quiet became a presence that demanded Patrick's attention. He looked up from his workbench, directly into the hooded eyes of

Benjamin Ranklin. Not knowing what to expect, he waited for Ranklin to start talking.

"Morning, Irish," Ranklin said.

"Morning Benjamin," Patrick stood. "What can I do for you?"

"Irish," he said, "I'd like to put some of the bad blood behind us."

"And how do you propose we do that?"

"We got off on the wrong foot," Ranklin said. "And I'd like to start over by using your services."

"What you got in mind?"

"I have need of milled lumber," he said, "if you'll give me a fair price."

"I'm sure I can cut what you need. And I'll bill you fair."

"Not sure how much I'll need." Ranklin slouched in the saddle. He didn't appear to be a threat, but Patrick kept an eye on him just the same.

"You need lumber for a barn or a house?"

"Need to build a house," Ranklin said. "That dirt floor cabin's getting long in the tooth. I'm gonna replace it. Looking to build a proper house."

"I'm sure your wife and son will be proud of a new home," Patrick said. "Will you need any assistance in building it?"

"Naw."

Ranklin was having trouble swallowing his pride, just in asking about the lumber. Someone had put in another mill over at Hagarville. It was surprising that Ranklin hadn't gone there first. Maybe he had. Most everybody said that Patrick's prices were better. No sense looking at things too closely though. Maybe this was a way to end the feud between the two clans.

"I can handle the building part myself," Ranklin said. "Get Jacob and a few neighbors to pitch in."

"I'd be glad to help," Patrick offered.

"I don't need your help!" Ranklin's back stiffened. "I can build a durn house. Just the lumber. That's all I need from you."

"Didn't mean nothing," Patrick bit at his cheek. "How soon do you need it?"

It was hard for Patrick not to take offense. Here he was just offering to help and Ranklin wanted to get snotty. Maybe the feud wasn't off after all.

He watched a dark cloud move across Ranklin's face before he got control of his emotions. After he settled down enough for normal conversation, Patrick helped him figure out the board footage, based on the dimensions of the planned house.

"If you can have some of it ready," Ranklin said. "I'll be back in two weeks to start gathering it up."

"I'll have the heavy stuff ready then," Patrick said. "Working your order in with what I've already got on the books will take a little longer. Cutting the planks will take the most time."

With that, Ranklin turned the appaloosa around and headed him toward Little Piney. Patrick watched him ride away until he could no longer be seen. A mountain lion might act peaceable enough as long as you were staring him down, but as soon as you turned your back, he might see his opportunity to attack.

Hans, too, had been watching the interaction from nearby. Once he was sure Ranklin was gone, he made his way to the workbench where Patrick had returned to his figures.

"That took a lot," he said.

"From him or me?" Patrick smiled.

"Both," Hans said. "Ben had to swallow a lot of pride to ask you for anything."

"I'm sure he did."

"And I know it took a lot from you," Hans said. "Not to tell him to go to hell."

"Took more for him than me, I figure."

Patrick scratched at the hair behind his right ear. Lost in thought, his face took on a concerned look. "I'll be as fair with a man as he'll let me be," Patrick said. "But, Ranklin's told himself I've stolen this land for so long, he truly believes it now."

"Maybe he'll get over it yet," Hans said.

"When I first looked up," Patrick gave a nervous, relieved laugh, "I thought the shooting was about to start."

"Still," Hans said. "You kept your wits about you. I'm proud of you."

"I appreciate that," Patrick said. "We'll just have to wait and see if I did the right thing."

"You're a good man, Patrick O'Brien," Hans said. "Sometimes though, you let people take advantage of you."

"I'll take that compliment," he smiled at Hans. "For a friend's eye is a good mirror."

"I think you did right," Hans said. "Most men wouldn't have."

"Maybe I should have told him to go to hell."

The two men went back to work, both wondering about the strange visit.

Ranklin rode back to Devil's Fork in silence with a smug look on his face. His next stop was his brother's place.

"Hello inside," he called out.

Jacob stepped from the dark shadows of his man-made cave. He was gnawing on a roasted leg of something that looked like it might have once been a turkey. Grease and crumbs flecked his beard.

"Where ya been?" Jacob asked.

"Been over to Irish's sawmill," Benjamin swung down from his horse.

"What the hell for?" Jacob's frown slowly turned into a grin as he imagined what could have taken place. "Didn't shoot the son-of-a-bitch did you?"

When Benjamin didn't answer right away Jacob wondered if maybe that's exactly what had transpired. His grin quickly flipped upside down again.

"You should have let me in on that."

"No, I didn't shoot him," Benjamin looked off up the trail toward his own cabin. "Ordered some lumber."

"What you need lumber for?"

"Gonna build me a house," Benjamin said. "Further back up the fork. Something proper for Caleb to grow up in."

"What you gonna do with the cabin?"

"Let it rot down."

"Can I have it?"

Jacob wasn't about to miss an opportunity to get something for nothing. If Benjamin was just going to pick up and move, why not take advantage of the windfall.

"It's better than this wet cave," he said. "And there'd be more room for Priscilla and her young'uns."

"Once I move out," Benjamin said. "I don't care what happens to it."

"How much did you have to pay Irish for the lumber?" Jacob didn't like the idea of doing business with O'Brien. He was having a tough time imagining his older brother doing business with him too. "Bet ya could have got it cheaper over in Hagarville."

"Me and Irish cut a deal," Benjamin turned toward his brother and grinned. "But that don't mean he'll ever see any of his money."

"Now you're talking like my brother," Jacob said. "I was beginning to worry about you."

"It's because of him that we ain't making no money," Benjamin said. "He's cut half the timber in the valley. That means fewer animals for our trap lines or commercial hunting."

"That's right," Jacob said. "No need to reward him for trying to run us out of business."

"Paying him," Benjamin reasoned aloud, "would be like paying for my own timber. That hollow belongs to me and so does everything in it."

"Too bad his good looking wench don't belong to us, eh?" Jacob looked around quickly to see who might have heard him. Not seeing anyone he continued. "Sure could have some fun with that one."

"Miss high and mighty," Benjamin spit the words. "Thinks she's too good for the likes of us."

"Maybe it's time she was taught a lesson," Jacob snorted.

"Her time will come," Benjamin said. "Her time will come."

24

Over the next couple of months, Ben brought wagon load after wagon load of lumber to his new building site near Owen's Creek. Slowly, the lumber was transformed into a house. While it was not up to the standard of many of the Little Piney Valley homes, it was head and shoulders above anything he'd ever lived in. It was also further away from any influence his brother's wild brood might have on his son Caleb.

"How much did all this lumber cost you?" asked John Dunlap.

A friend of the Ranklin's, John Dunlap helped with some of the building chores. He knew a little about framing and keeping walls mostly square. Benjamin, Jacob, and he were celebrating the completion of the house with a jug of sour-mash whiskey.

"Ain't cost me nuthin," Benjamin admitted. "That damn Irish stole all that timber from me, to begin with. I'm just letting him cut up my own timber for me." He grinned and passed the celebration jug. Jacob took it and took a deep pull at its golden contents.

"What you mean?" asked Dunlap. "How'd he steal it?"

"He talked the government into giving him my land," Benjamin said. "I'm the one that discovered this valley. And I bought it all, fair and square. Irish and them other foreigners convinced the government to take it from me and give it to them."

Jacob pulled a tomahawk from his belt. It was of the type Benjamin had used in his trading days with the Indians. A simple, forged ax head, with a hardwood handle. The handle was decorated with two rows of brass nails driven into each side of the handle. Something the Osage preferred. He hefted the tomahawk in his hand and drawing back, threw it end over end at the butt end of a gum stump. It struck a glancing blow and bounced off into the dirt.

"O'Brien told me he bought that hollow from a land speculator in New York." Dunlap walked over to retrieve the small ax.

"Hell, everybody knows you can't trust an Irishman," Benjamin spit, taking the tomahawk from Dunlap. "They'll lie about anything. Probably saying he give me a good price on that lumber too."

"I did hear that," Dunlap hesitated to add.

"The Irish thief overcharged me on that lumber, he did." Benjamin's sharp rebuke was affected by the amount of corn mash he'd already consumed. "That is if I was going to agree to such robbery. I'll be hanged if he'll ever see one red cent!"

Benjamin aimed the tomahawk, slobber hanging in the corner of his mouth. He gave the tomahawk a sharp, twisting throw. It struck the end of the stump with a solid thump. He turned and grinned at Jacob.

"He overcharged me on lumber too," Jacob shook his head in disgust. "He ain't nothing but a cheat."

"I've never known you to buy any lumber," Dunlap said. "You got some construction project going on that I don't know about."

"Go to hell, Dunlap," Jacob snarled. "You don't know all my business. Fetch the tomahawk."

"Jacob's just making a point," Benjamin cut in. "What Jacob has and hasn't bought ain't the issue here. The point is that Irish will cheat anyone. He just can't be trusted."

"I knew Jacob liberated a little lumber once," Dunlap snorted. "I's with him. Some posts walked off from Göbel's place and got sold down in Union. Got enough to buy some of that German's wine. Might say it was bought with his own money."

Dunlap started laughing but Jacob didn't seem to see the humor in what he'd said. "I ain't never stole nothing from nobody." His eyes clouded as he jerked the tomahawk from Dunlap's hand. "And I'll gut any bastard that says I did."

"Take it easy," Dunlap backtracked. "I's just funning. Don't take things so personal."

"Jacob's right," Benjamin cut back into the conversation. "We Ranklin's don't steal. Never have. Wish the same could be said for Irish."

"He ain't nothing but a drunken thief," Jacob added. He poked the tomahawk back into his belt and punctuated his words by turning up the jug of whiskey. He passed the jug to Benjamin, who took a swig and passed it back to Dunlap.

"What needs to be done," Benjamin looked hard at Dunlap. "Is word needs to get around just how sorry Irish is."

"That's what our friends ought to be saying," Jacob said. "Irish is a liar."

"There was a time," Benjamin said, "when people came to me for things. Questions about where the best land was for farming; where the best fishing might be; where to get a bear or turkey; secrets of this valley; such as that. Now people seem to be seeking out the opinion of Irish and that damn German."

"My brother's opinion should be the only one that counts in his own valley," Jacob affirmed.

"But it isn't his valley." Dunlap knew he'd said too much when Benjamin's black eyes locked on his own. Like a dog caught stealing eggs, he wilted under Benjamin's scolding gaze. "But we all know it should be," Dunlap added quickly.

"That's what we're saying," Benjamin said.

A chilled breeze swept down Devil's Fork as if to emphasize the mountain man's words.

"This was my valley," he continued. "Especially, everything north of the junction of Devil's Fork and Little Piney. That includes Cliffy Hollow. And one day soon, it will be mine again."

"What about O'Brien?" asked Dunlap. "What if he won't sell it to you? What if he claims you owe him for that lumber and comes looking for payment?"

"Oh, I won't *ask* him to sell me what's mine, ever again," Benjamin smiled. "And I hope he does come demanding money from me. With him dead, there won't be anybody to say that hollow ain't mine."

"Then maybe people will start respecting my brother and me," Jacob said. "We're the Bull of the Woods in these parts."

"I know people who's come on hard times," Dunlap said. "They say O'Brien let 'em slide on paying. What if he don't come demanding payment?"

"What kind of a lily-livered skunk wouldn't want his money?" asked Jacob.

"I was just asking."

"One way or another," Benjamin said. "This will get decided. Once and for all."

25

Ranklin's plan wasn't working. Patrick wasn't demanding payment. And he wasn't getting upset with all the loose talk about him being a cheat. People were considering the source, so he just ignored it. That made Ranklin even madder.

"Ben is a scalawag," Hans Göbel told Patrick. "He's got no intention of ever paying you."

"Don't worry about it, Hans."

"He acts like everybody owes *him*," Hans said. "Got a high opinion of himself 'cause he saw this valley first. Thinks everyone should kowtow to him."

"Don't really matter what Ranklin thinks about himself," Patrick said. "What matters is what others think."

"Well, I don't think he has any intention of paying you."

"He'll pay when he has the money."

Patrick wasn't sure if Ranklin would pay or not. But he would give him the benefit of the doubt. A man should be considered honest until he proved himself otherwise. Even though his past actions didn't indicate he could be trusted with much.

"Maybe Ranklin's going through a rough patch," he said.

"Rough patch my eye," Hans said. "If he knew he couldn't pay, he shouldn't have ordered all that lumber."

"There's not as much game around as there once was," Patrick said. "Could be his commercial hunting business is off."

"There's plenty of game around." Hans couldn't sit any longer. Full of nervous energy, he stood up waved his hands in the air to make his point. "I've heard him with my own ears," Hans said. "Down in Union, I overheard him tell Jessie Clark that you'd overcharged him and he wasn't ever going to pay you."

"My business is doing very well," Patrick tried to sooth Hans' ruffled feathers. "My family isn't going to go hungry if Benjamin Ranklin doesn't pay right away. I can afford to give him some time."

"What if he don't pay you at all?" Hans demanded. "What if he intended to cheat you all along?"

"If he can live with it—I can live without it."

"We both know he hates you," Hans was mad even if Patrick wasn't. "He's taking advantage of your generous heart and calling you a coward to boot. 'Cause you won't confront him about payment."

"He wouldn't be the first."

"Make light if you want," Hans said. "But I've heard him talk down on you more'n once. He's jealous!"

"Jealous?" Patrick laughed. "What makes you think he's jealous of me?"

"You work hard for everything you get," Hans said, "and he tells everyone you're a cheat. Your neighbors respect you and ask for your opinion on things. Nobody asks him about anything. He claims your timber cutting is running off all the game. And, at the end of the day, he just plain don't like the Irish. He considers you his enemy, yah!"

"Like I've said before. Let the Devil cut off the toes of all our foes," Patrick smiled at his friend. "That we may know them by their limping."

"Yea, I know," said Hans. "But you'd best cut out the limericks. He ain't ever gonna pay you," Hans shook his head. "He's spoiling for a fight."

Patrick could see that his easy-going attitude was just upsetting Hans. The lighter he tried to make of it, the more upset Hans got.

"If Benjamin Ranklin wants to confront me about some wrong he feels I've done," Patrick said. "Let him face me man to man."

"Face to face ain't gonna happen," Hans warned. "Neither him, nor his brother, Jacob, are going to face a man in a fair fight. Not if there's a possibility for shooting 'em in the back."

"Then I'll have to keep my eyes open."

Patrick tried to put the conversation out of his mind. If Ranklin wanted trouble, he knew where to find it. Patrick wasn't going looking for it. He had work enough to occupy his mind. That and a loving family to tend to. With four growing children, Helen needed all his spare time.

That's when real trouble found the peaceful Little Piney Valley. During the humid, dog days of August, it happened. Something the valley had long feared. On a day just like any other day, a small wagon train entered the valley. With them came the pox.

In the dry days of late summer, the pox ignited and swept through the valley like a prairie fire. Every family was touched by it in some way. Those not directly affected by the illness had close friends who were. People got sick, ran high fevers, and some succumbed to the disease. Six children died from it that August. And, in a roundabout way, so did Helen O'Brien.

Some felt the infected wagon train should never have been allowed to enter the valley. Those who lost loved ones looked for someplace to lay the blame. The disease continued to spread. No one knew how to stop it. Wagging tongues said that the only way to stop it was to burn it out.

One Sunday, after services at the Methodist church, a large group of residents stuck around after services to discuss their problems. They were desperate for answers.

"I'm telling you," Jacob Ranklin seemed the loudest. "Fire's the only way!"

The Ranklin's weren't regular attendees inside the church house like their wives were. They did like to wait out around the wagon yard with other men. That's where they passed around the brown jug and figured out all the gossip.

"That's probably true," Patrick said. "You can't get rid of it with cedar boughs. Best way to get rid of it is by burning the bedding and clothing and such."

In the slums of New York, he'd seen this kind of hysteria before. The end result was usually worse than the problem.

"We can burn the wagons and all the bedclothes from the sick ones," someone offered.

"But what would you do about the cabins where there are sick ones now?" Patrick asked. "They need a place to stay."

"Burn 'em to the ground!" Jacob growled.

"What about the people in those houses?" Hans confronted Jacob's hysteria. "Where would they live, if you burn their wagons and cabins?"

"Burn them with it," Benjamin took up his brother's call. "Anything to protect my family."

For those assembled, this was going too far. Things were getting out of hand.

"You're talking crazy," Patrick said. He knew he couldn't make either Ranklin see reason and they were just going to keep agitating. He turned to leave and the little knot of men around him decided it was time to go as well.

As wagons and riders left the churchyard, Benjamin called after them, "Jacob's right! Fire's the only answer!"

26

An immigrant family was the scapegoat for the panic caused by the pox epidemic. A young man, his wife, and small infant arrived with a wagon train on its way through the valley, headed further north. All three had the pox.

Too weak to travel on, they'd settled temporarily into a ramshackle, lean-to of a cabin, back in the woods near Gobblers Point. Here they were isolated, away from the larger community.

That next Sunday morning, the preacher told his congregation of the young family's plight. "This family needs our prayers," he expounded from the pulpit. "Furthermore, they need our assistance. Any help you can offer will be appreciated."

After the services, the men gathered in the wagon yard arguing once again about how best to control the spread of the pox. The women gathered at the front of the church and had their own discussion.

"What do we need to do?" Helen asked.

"I carried them a poultice yesterday," Elizabeth Göbel said. "It should help. But they're awful weak. They need someone to cook for them. Someone especially needs to help with that baby. Is there anyone who can take her in?"

"Not me," said Mary Shaw.

"And bring the pox into my own home?" said Judy Gatlin. "Huh! No way."

"I'd do it myself," Elizabeth said, "but there are too many families that need doctoring. I can't be that far out of the way."

"What if I went over there and helped?" asked Helen. "I was exposed back in Five Points. I caught it then and made it through it. I don't think you can catch it twice."

"You'd have to stay over there." Concern crept into Elizabeth's voice. "You wouldn't want to take a chance of carrying it home to your own. You got four little ones you wouldn't want exposed."

"It would just be for a few days." Helen was already planning it in her head. It would be hard to convince Patrick it was the right thing to do. "Patrick could handle things for that long," Helen told Elizabeth. "And you could drop in and check on them every so often."

"You're taking a big chance," Lela Harrison said.

"I don't know if I like this idea," Elizabeth began.

"It'll be fine." Helen cut her off before she could try to talk her out of it. She started for her own wagon. Looking over her shoulder, she smiled at Elizabeth. "I'll go home and get some things ready. Patrick can take me over there this evening."

Elizabeth wanted to protest, but everyone drifted away to their families. The men broke up and got wagons ready to leave. From their haste, it appeared some of the men had important matters on their mind—probably Sunday dinner. In short order, the churchyard was empty.

True to her word, and over Patrick's protests, Helen moved in with the sick couple that afternoon. Over the next few days, Elizabeth checked on her friend often, bringing food and poultices. By the end of the week, it appeared that the infant was recovering. Unfortunately, her parents were getting worse.

"How's the little girl?" Elizabeth was busy applying a poultice to the young man's chest.

"She's in bad need of a wet nurse. But we're not going to find anyone willing to take that chance," Helen was cradling the baby in her arms. "Last night I finally got her pacified with a sugar-tit."

"Looks like you're doing fine with her," Elizabeth said. "What did you find to put the sugar in?"

"I had to use my silk handkerchief," Helen said. "It was the only thing I could find that was clean. Wouldn't want the little thing trying to suck sugar through a wool sock."

Elizabeth took Helen by the arm and led her into the yard. Concern was evident on her face. She started talking in a low voice. "I don't like the looks of those two," she said. She didn't want the couple inside to hear her. Although in their fevered condition it was an unnecessary precaution.

"They're both in bad shape," she said. "Don't look like they're going to make it."

"How long before we know for sure?" Helen asked.

"I'm surprised they made it this long. If they weren't so young, they'd probably already be gone."

"Is there anything more I can do?"

"You're already doing all that can be done," Elizabeth hesitated before continuing. "Only time will tell. But you keep a lookout."

"What do you mean?" Helen didn't understand. "Keep a lookout for what?"

"There's talk in the valley," Elizabeth said. "Especially coming from them Ranklin brothers."

"What kind of talk?" Helen could see the concern in Elizabeth's eyes.

"They're still talking about burning the pox out of this valley," Elizabeth said. "It's probably just talk, but you keep an eye out."

"It's just a bunch of pop and blow."

27

"What we going to do about this pox?" John Dunlap asked.

"What are you going to do about it?" Benjamin Ranklin replied. "Just like the rest of this valley, you're going to wring your hands and do nothing."

The Ranklin brothers were sitting on the bank of Little Piney fishing with their friend John Dunlap. None of them were seriously trying to catch anything. It was just an excuse to lay around in a cool spot and drink.

"But something needs to be done," Dunlap said.

"Jacob and I have done told everybody that'll listen," Benjamin said. "The only way to stop the pox is to burn it out."

"Burn it out," Jacob repeated. "It's the only way."

Dunlap picked up a fist-sized rock and threw it out into the stream. It struck with a plunk, sending a small column of water into the air. It splashed back down, creating a series of water rings that grew ever larger. Benjamin gave him a disgusted look.

"You're scaring the fish."

"That wagon train came through Hagarville," Dunlap meekly sat back down. "Ain't none of them caught it," he pouted.

"That's 'cause they passed *through* Hagarville," Jacob whined. "We let them pilgrims stop here."

"Them pilgrims are now our problem," Benjamin said. "Them and the O'Brien's. That's our real problem."

"What's the O'Brien's got to do with this?" asked Dunlap. "They didn't bring pox into the valley."

"Didn't say they brung it," Benjamin grunted. "Do you know you're dumb as a post?"

Dunlap opened his mouth to object.

"Yeah," Jacob filled the silence. "Dumb! Like a post."

"Them wandering pilgrims brought it," Benjamin explained. "But they'd a kept on going, and took it with 'em, if them O'Brien's hadn't took them under their wing."

"But them folks in that cabin on Gobblers Point couldn't have gone on. They were too sick to travel and their wagon train had already left them behind. That's when Mrs. O'Brien showed them sympathy and offered a little human comfort," Dunlap eyebrows knitted into a question. "Don't you think she's just being Christian?"

"You think it Christian to hold the pox here until everyone in the valley has it?" Jacob spit the accusation.

"I don't think..." Dunlap got out before he was interrupted.

"That's right," Benjamin said. "You don't think. Just like most of the people in this valley. All anybody can do is swoon when that red-headed witch casts her spells. She's got every man smitten and every woman fooled."

"She is easy to look at," Dunlap agreed. "Best looking woman in two counties. But what's that got to do with..."

"See there," Jacob pointed his finger at Dunlap. "She's got you under her spell too."

"Well," Dunlap defended his feelings. "I think Mrs. O'Brien is doing a fine thing, helping that young family and all. She's always looking out for unfortunates. That's why folks respect her."

"Miss High and Mighty may soon get her comeuppance," Benjamin said. "What's she going to do when she spreads the pox to her friends? Or to that red-freckled brood of hers? She going to burn down her own cabin, with them in it?"

"Why we got to burn things?" Dunlap asked.

"That's the only thing that'll stop the pox, fool," Jacob said.

"Where there's pox, you burn everything. Clothes, bed, belongs. Everything. That includes wherever folks was staying when they died from it. Cabin, wagon, or tent."

"If them pilgrims die in that Gobbler's Point cabin," Dunlap said. "Then we'll have to burn it down I guess."

"Yeah," Benjamin said. "Guess we'll just have to burn it down."

28

Before Elizabeth left, Helen tried to reassure her friend, as well as herself, that the gossip about the Ranklin's causing trouble was just talk. "I'm sure it's nothing to worry about."

"Well, I got to get on back," Elizabeth glanced back toward the cabin. "Patrick said to tell you he'd be by first thing in the morning." Sadness soaked Elizabeth's face. "I don't hold out much hope for them two," she said. "They could go any day now."

"I'll keep a close watch on them."

"I'll pray for them—and for you," Elizabeth patted Helen on her arm. "You're an angel."

"I do look forward to seeing Patrick tomorrow," Helen said. "But I really miss my babies the most."

"They miss you too," Elizabeth said. "This should be over soon."

"Don't you tell Patrick I miss the children most," Helen smiled. "He might get jealous."

"I won't," Elizabeth said. "He wouldn't believe it anyway."

"Until I see you again," Helen called as Elizabeth drove the wagon out of the yard.

Elizabeth looked back once before she lost sight of the cabin in the pine trees. Helen stood silhouetted in the cabin door, her red hair waving gently in the evening breeze, her right hand extended in a sisterly goodbye.

After it was dark, Helen banked the fire for the night. It was warm and there was no need for the heat. She checked on the husband and wife. Both were resting quietly. Their fever was still high, but they weren't as fitful as they had been.

The baby was a different matter. It took Helen a long time to get the baby settled down. She was fighting sleep, but her fever had finally broken. It was late in the night before the baby drifted off.

Helen placed the baby in a makeshift crib, a discarded wooden feed-trough lined with tattered blankets. Draping a shawl around her own shoulders, Helen sat down next to the fireplace. She drifted off into her own restless slumber.

Around midnight, a noise startled her awake. At first, she wasn't sure she'd really heard anything. A quick glance around the room showed nothing amiss. The moonlight, filtering through the only window, revealed that the baby was still sleeping. The dark bulk of the man and woman lying on the corn shuck bed didn't appear to have moved.

"The sound didn't come from inside," Helen said aloud. "It sounded like it was on the roof."

But there was nothing now.

"Must have been a raccoon or a flying squirrel," she said to the night.

Hearing nothing else, she pulled the shawl up around her and was soon fast asleep.

She awoke to a room full of smoke. A popping and crackling sound came from somewhere above. Choking and gasping for breath, she felt her way to the couple on the bed. When she touched them, she knew from their cold, stiff feel that they were dead. The disease had already claimed their sweet lives. A quick check for a pulse confirmed her suspicions.

Not thinking, she stood quickly and turned toward the crib. As her head entered the poisonous cloud of smoke, its acrid fumes overcame her and she collapsed, knocking the crib over, spilling its contents to the floor. She struggled for consciousness, trying to cough the blistering smoke from her lungs.

Crawling across the dirt floor, she felt frantically for the baby. In the dark, she followed the sound of crying until her fingers found the bundle of swaddling clothes. Sinking her fingers into the blanket, she gathered it to her and began crawling desperately for the door.

29

Just inside the burned-out doorway is where the neighbors found Helen the next morning. Overcome, she and the baby died only inches away from fresh air and salvation. The infant's parents were found under the smoldering debris.

"I saw smoke against the skyline when I went out to milk." One neighbor said to the others who had gathered.

"Figured it must be coming from here."

"Wonder what started it?"

"Sparks from the chimney must have caught the roof."

"Boy howdy, I wouldn't want to be the one that had to tell her husband."

"I wouldn't want to be the one that had to tell her kids."

"You won't have to worry about telling Patrick, here he comes now."

Those assembled turned to see Patrick and the Göbel's coming through the woods. From the rock-strewn trail, it was impossible to take in the scene until they broke out into the clearing surrounding the cabin. But they had seen the smoke plume rising over the treetops from miles away.

Patrick tried to brace himself for what he might find. But he hadn't dared to imagine just how devastating it would be.

Elizabeth turned from the scene, burying her head in Hans' chest.

"OH GOD! No!"

Patrick said nothing. He made his way to the cabin door and fell on his knees, his legs no longer able to support him. Taking Helen's soot-covered face in his lap, he began to rock and sob. It was an hour before he was able to compose himself enough to wrap his wife in a blanket and place her gently in the back of the Göbel's wagon.

"I'm taking her back home," he told Hans. Turning to Elizabeth, his voice cracked. "We'll prepare the body there."

Elizabeth nodded.

"How am I going to tell them?" Patrick sobbed. "How?"

It was a long trip back to Cliffy Hollow. Once there, Patrick and Elizabeth carried the body to the large room and began to clean and dress her.

"I don't want the children to see her," Patrick said, "until she's been washed and dressed proper."

Elizabeth agreed. Hans, with the help of a few neighbor women, kept the children occupied down at the millpond until Helen had been washed and dressed in her best calico dress. Then Patrick brought them into the family room and sat holding them until late in the night.

The wake only lasted long enough for the men to dig a proper grave in the rocky soil on the hillside west of the house.

After the burial, it was hard for the younger children to understand that Helen wouldn't be coming back.

Connell and Killian were old enough to understand Mama wasn't just gone off somewhere for another visit.

What Timothy and Josephine knew was that she had been gone for the last few days. She was taking care of some sick people. When she did come home, she lay sleeping in the big room and couldn't be disturbed. Then Papa and some other men brought this box outside and buried it on the knoll. There had been some sad talk about all Mama did, and how important she was, and that she was going to be missed. There were lots of tears. Then everyone went home.

Now Mama was gone again. They overheard people speaking of gone to a better place, but they weren't sure where that was; someplace from which she couldn't return. The women especially were saying it was going to be hard on the children. It would be hard on them. Especially hard on five-year-old Josephine.

"When is Mama coming home?" she asked Patrick. "I want Mama."

"Come here, baby."

He gathered her into his arms and reached out to the three boys. He pulled them together in a big hug. Through tear-soaked eyes, he told them how much their mother loved them.

He tried to explain how God had needed another angel, and He wanted the best. Patrick tried to explain the unexplainable. Unexplainable, because he couldn't understand it himself. Why would a loving God take such a perfect Mother from her children?

The first night after the funeral was the worst on the children. The youngest was five and the oldest only ten.

They needed their mother. It would be quite some time before they would quit asking for her.

Elizabeth had tried to put them to bed earlier. But Patrick heard them crying. He slipped across the hall and knelt beside their bed.

"What's wrong with my babies?"

"I'm scared," said little Timothy. "I want Mama to sing me a lullaby and hold my hand."

"Uh hu," Josephine agreed from around the thumb stuck in her mouth.

Tears flooded Patrick's eyes anew. "Mothers hold their children's hands for just a little while," he told his children, "and their hearts forever."

For a long time that was all he could choke past the restriction in his throat. He lay down beside them and when he could talk again, he did his best to hum a lullaby.

It was the one he'd heard Helen sing to their children on stormy nights. All five O'Brien's huddled together in the same bed—each needing to touch and to be touched. The whippoorwills had long since stopped calling by the time the children drifted off to a fitful sleep.

Daylight found Patrick still awake. The O'Brien's had lost the most important person in their lives. But they still had her memory. And one other thing—each other.

The next night Patrick started a tradition he would repeat for the rest of his life. The spot Patrick picked for Helen's grave was just west of the house. It sat upon the brow of a small hill. It had been his habit, after supper, to walk out on the back porch for a smoke. Usually, Helen would join him there to watch the sunset and plan for the future.

With Helen's death, that had all changed. For him, there was no future. Only the dull responsibility of getting through another day. If not for the bright spot of the children she had given him, he'd crawl into a jug and drown his worries. Maybe even drown more than that.

But the children needed him. So he would look to the setting sun—to the oak on the hill—and see only the past. As long as the sun continued to set in the west, he and Helen would meet in the gathering dusk. In his mind, he would take her by her hand and he'd tell her all the things her children had done that day. In the magic time suspended between light and dark, between real and imagined, they would have their time.

30

One day turned into two, then a week passed, then months, then years. The children grew and Patrick went through the motion of living. He did what he had to do and little more. One numb day routinely became another. Such was the case this day. It started just like so many before.

The first light of morning wasn't even a promise when Patrick O'Brien awoke. "It's time to be rising," he called out to his boys. "The devil loves idle hands."

Patrick had made a deal with the Langley's on Gillian Mountain. They had a large stand of oaks they wanted cut and milled into heavy timbers and 1 x 6 boards. Patrick had felled the trees, skidded them up onto wagons, and then transported them to his sawmill by ox teams. It had taken a couple of weeks to mill the logs into the desired lumber.

Today, he and Connell would return to Gillian Settlement with the first load of lumber. It would be an all-day job and Patrick wanted to get an early start.

The Langley's wanted to build a nice home, one they hoped would be the talk of the valley. They wanted multiple roof lines with wrap-around porches and a wide entryway. They had seen Patrick's earlier work and were impressed. They were considering having him build the house, too. Business had fallen off lately, and it was work he needed.

"Connell, shake them covers," Patrick said.

At sixteen, Connell was turning into a steady hand. He was a man Patrick could count on. He was learning the mill business, knew how to figure lumber while it was still standing, and was becoming a craftsman with hand tools.

"It's time we get a wiggle on."

"Coming, Papa!"

Connell stretched and swung his legs over the edge of his bed. The hardwood floor felt rough to his bare feet as he searched for his boots.

With a lot of yawning and scratching, the three boys made their way downstairs and set about their early chores by lantern light. Josephine too made her way out to the chicken house. At eleven, she had taken over some of the duties that had once been her mothers. Helping prepare breakfast for the family was one of them and it would come immediately after the early chores were done.

This was the time of day Patrick missed Helen most. He still went to talk with her in the evening, needed her at night, but it was the early morning that reminded him most of his loss.

"I'll get the bacon frying," Patrick said. "You young'uns hustle up."

Patrick had heard widowers talk of missing a wife most during the dark hours of bedtime. Patrick had found that not to be true. Sure, he missed the private time shared by a man and woman. Missed her touch and smell. But what he missed most was starting a new day with her.

Even now, his mind could hear her preparing breakfast while he busied himself with morning chores. He could hear the coffee pot being filled with water from the gourd in the bucket. The clink of the flat spoon striking the edge of the cast-iron skillet. He remembered returning to a house floating with the aroma of bacon, coffee, and his Helen.

He remembered how sometimes he would step inside from a foggy autumn morning, a cool bite to the air, and she would already be preparing a dessert that she would have ready by suppertime. It had been seven years since he'd lost her, but it was still hard. It might be the smell of honeysuckle or even vanilla extract she daubed behind her ear, that could bring on her memory and the crying binge that usually accompanied the remembered loss. She'd been the air he breathed, the marrow in his bones.

Patrick brought himself back to the present. He was determined not to start another day with tears. He had coffee on the stove, biscuits in the Dutch oven, and bacon sizzling in the pan when Connell came back in from the barn.

"Did you give them oxen a portion of oats and molasses?" he asked.

"Sure did, Papa," Connell replied. "Knew you'd expect a hard day's work out of 'em. Gotta feed 'em if you expect to work 'em. That's what you always say."

"That's right," Patrick said. "Be it man or beast, you can't work on a belly full of grass. A working animal deserves a good feed, you ready for yours?"

"I'm sure hungry," Connell agreed. "But that don't mean I gotta pull them wagons by myself does it?"

"There's times you're as stubborn as an ox."

Patrick felt a smile tug at the corners of his mouth as he reached over and caught Connell by the bicep. He jokingly felt of the muscle then shook his head. "Naw, I think I better keep the oxen for the heavy stuff."

Connell laughed and headed to the wash pan to wash his face and hands.

"Has Killian milked that cow?"

"Yes, sir. Milks right here," Killian chirped as he walked in the door with a heavy pail. White milk splashed over its brim and sloshed onto the hardwood floor. Using a gourd dipper, Killian poured a mug of milk for each of the three younger family members.

"Tim's slopping the hogs," Killian volunteered.

"What about little Joe?" Patrick asked. He couldn't help but smile, thinking of an incident that happened with a rooster, two days earlier. "She got them eggs yet?"

Josephine had been flogged by the rooster. She'd been minding her own business out in the yard when the rooster decided to declare his territory. But the red-headed rooster met his match from another red-head with green eyes.

The rooster had attacked Josephine, its neck feathers standing on end, spurs slashing, and wings flopping. The eleven-year-old child had ducked out of the way, receiving only a few scratches. Calmly, she walked back around the house. From the porch, she picked up the Chocktaw *rabbit stick* her brothers had been teaching her to use.

Made of hickory, it was approximately fifteen inches long. One end was rough with the bark still on it. The other end had been whittled down to a handle. Hard and heavy, it was a stick used for throwing. In the hands of someone skilled in its use, it was a deadly weapon for hunting small game.

Josephine eased around the house until she spotted the rooster strutting around a group of hens. As she stepped out from the corner of the house, the rooster spotted her. He began to fuzz-up and strut, in anticipation of attacking her again. In one smooth motion, Josephine drew back and threw the rabbit stick as hard as she could. Her aim was true.

Patrick remembered that although it was tough, the chicken dinner they'd had that night had tasted pretty good.

"She's still in the henhouse," Connell said.

He tried to suppress the laugh building inside. "If one of them hen's peck her, maybe we'll have another chicken dinner." Killian laughed out loud, spitting milk down the front of his shirt.

"What's so funny?" Timothy asked as he came in from feeding the hogs.

"Never mind," Patrick tried to be stern, but it wasn't working. "You boys get her Irish up—she'll be fetching a rabbit stick upside your head."

All three boys began to laugh. Patrick couldn't help but join in.

"You four are awful happy this early in the morning," Josephine marched into the kitchen. "I could hear you laughing all the way out in the yard."

"Sit down and have your breakfast," Patrick soothed. "You find many eggs?"

The boys began to snicker milk out their noses again.

31

During breakfast, Patrick laid out the plans for the day. He and Connell would be working over at the Gillian Settlement, and it would be near dark when they got back.

"Killian, you and Timothy hoe the weeds out of the corn," he said. "Joe, you stay near the house and clean up a bit."

"Yes, Papa," all three said without a lot of enthusiasm.

"I expect a clean house and clean rows when I get back," Patrick said.

"If'n we get through in time," Timothy asked, "kin we go fishin', Papa?"

"Only after them chores are done," Patrick said. He stood and reached for his hat hanging near the kitchen door. Setting it lightly on his head, he thought to add. "You boys watch out for your sister while we're gone."

"Yes sir," both boys mumbled in unison.

With that, Patrick and Connell headed out the door for the barn where they harnessed the team of oxen by lantern light. When it was light enough for chickens to fly down, they were well on their way to Gillian Settlement. By midday, they were well into their work, thoughts of home far from their minds.

Back in Cliffy Hollow, Josephine fed chops and crushed corn to the chickens. Then she washed up the morning dishes and swept out the house. She made up the beds, except for Patrick's. Patrick took care of that chore himself. That is when it needed doing. More often than not, he didn't sleep in his bed. Instead, he'd sit up all night in a chair, catching little cat naps and thinking about Helen. He still found it hard to go to bed without her.

After making the beds, Josephine went out to the smokehouse. There she trimmed slices of meat from a cured ham. She planned to warm it up and serve it to her brothers for lunch.

Killian and Timothy went down to the mill race and brought buckets of freshwater up to the house. Next, they headed to the barn and threw fresh hay down from the loft. Then they sharpened their hoes and chopped weeds out of the corn.

The sun marched steadily upward in its daily trek, warming the day up nicely. Dew burned off the corn shoots quickly, leaving behind the dusty smell of dirt with each chop of the hoe. At the end of one of the rows, the boys paused to catch their breath and wipe at sweat.

"What we should be doing is marking some hogs," Killian suggested.

"I don't think so," said Timothy. "Papa didn't say nothing about us doing that."

Killian propped on his hoe handle watching a grasshopper chew on a leaf. His face suddenly lit up. "He didn't say we couldn't do it," excitement tinged his voice.

"We'll get in trouble," Timothy warned.

"We could take Ol' Blue."

Killian continued planning as if Timothy hadn't said a thing. "We could go down near the Little Piney bottoms. It'd be cool in there. Blue can catch the shoats and hold them by the ear while we mark them. Papa and Connell don't have the time to do it right now—and it needs doing."

"You're right. I heard Papa say that it needed doing," Timothy gave in.

"Yeah," Killian said. "We could have us some fun!"

"It would be fun," Timothy agreed. "You think Blue would mind us?" Timothy asked. "He's partial to Papa you know."

"Once we get the scent of hogs in his nose, he'll do what comes natural."

"What about Joe?" Indecision crept back into Timothy's voice. "Papa told us to watch out for her."

"We'll tell her to stay close to the house," Killian said.

"Yeah. She won't be in no danger there," Timothy agreed.

"But the roosters might be," Killian laughed out loud at his own joke.

"What if she don't stay at the house," Timothy said. "She don't like being bossed by us," he continued. "We could get in some real trouble."

"We'll tell her that when we get back, we'll take her swimmin!"

"I still don't know," Timothy said.

"She'll be okay," Killian said.

"Yeah, she'll be fine," Timothy agreed. "Let's do it."

With that, both boys raced back to the barn. Suddenly they weren't tired anymore. They threw a blanket on the mare and placed a halter over her head. As Timothy walked the mare out of the lot, Killian came bounding out of the house with his papa's double-barreled shotgun and a sharp hunting knife.

"Where do you two think you're off to with that shotgun?" Joe called from the front porch.

"Never you mind," Killian called over his shoulder. "We got business to take care of."

"We'll be back shortly," said Timothy. "Then we're going swimmin'."

"You jest be ready to go swimmin' when we get back," Killian slapped his thigh. "Come on Blue."

Boys, dog, and horse all headed out of the yard, past the walnut trees, and down the road toward the river.

"You be ready when we git back," Killian called, reminding Joe of his tempting promise.

32

"Killian," Timothy kicked at a clod of dirt. "How come hogs mostly live out in the woods? But then they's some that stays up around people's houses?"

"I ain't never given it much thought," Killian replied.

"I've heard talk about wild mustangs that run free out West. Heard grownups talk about wild cattle down in Texas. But for the most part, around here, livestock is kept under fence up near a barn or something," Timothy continued. "But hogs, whether they belong to somebody or not, just roam free. Most stay in the bottoms and canebrakes. Only way you know who they belong to is by the earmarks that folks cut into their ears. Other hogs stay up in the yard and hardly ever go out into the woods. It don't make sense. Why are hogs different?"

"Hogs ain't meant for penning," Killian started, then hesitated. "They's kinda like people."

"Like people?"

"Sure. Some people, and some hogs, are lazy. That's them you find up near a house," Killian spoke like the older brother that he was. And being older, he had to know all the answers so he could explain things to his younger brother. "Then they's others whut cain't sit still. Always gotta see what's over that next hill."

"You're talking crazy."

"Them lazy ones are always looking for an easy meal," Killian said. "Up near the house, somebody's gonna feed 'em." Killian thought ahead, and what he was about to tell

Timothy made sense. Maybe it was true, maybe it wasn't. "They got it too good where they's at," he said.

"Got it too good," Timothy shook his head. "How you figger? We fatten 'em up, then when the first good cold spell comes along, we butcher 'em and hang 'em in the smokehouse."

"Hogs don't know they's gonna get butchered, now do they?" Killian looked at Timothy as if he were dumber than a sack of rocks. "Anyway, who's telling this story?"

"You're telling it," Timothy said. "That don't mean I'm believing it. That's probably just what it is—a story."

"Just think about it," Killian said. "Them house hogs waller out a good mud hole in the shade, git slopped once or twice a day, and just lay around raising flies." He looked at Timothy and nodded his head up and down to make his point. Timothy nodded his head too, showing he understood so far.

"Yep," Killian continued. "They got the life, they do. Why, I've seen some folks let 'em come in the house, anytime they want."

"Ain't neither!"

"Swear!" Killian raised his left hand in the air. "Ol' man Isom got one sleeps in the cabin with him."

Timothy was cutting sideways looks at Killian. This was beginning to sound too much like one of Hans Göbel's tall tales.

"Some folks say they sleep in the same bed," Killian added.

"I've seen ol' man Isom's place," Timothy scoffed. "It ain't much of a cabin anyway."

"Never you mind. I'm telling you the straight of it."

Timothy wanted to argue, but he knew it wouldn't do any good. Even if it wasn't true, Killian was going to stick to his story now. He was committed.

"Them hogs what got the wanderlust," Killian warmed to his work. "Well, you couldn't build a corral strong enough to hold 'em. Them's the ones what runs off and raises in the bottoms and canebrakes, living off acorns and snakes."

"But them that live in the woods all the time," Timothy asked, "they's wild ain't they?"

"Some is, some ain't." Killian had an idea. "Remember that man talking to Papa about them razorbacks?"

"The man from over around Union?" asked Timothy.

"That's the one. He said them razorbacks are out of Russian boar stock. And they's wild!" Killian scratched at the side of his jaw as if pondering the man's statement. Then he nodded his head in agreement. "Them razorbacks are tough all right," he said. "All they know is wild ways."

"Then maybe we best leave 'em alone," Timothy said. He was beginning to lose his nerve again. This was beginning to sound more like trouble than some great adventure.

"Them razorbacks will leave us alone unless'n they's cornered," Killian said. He stopped in the middle of the road and looked Timothy straight in the eye. "What we got to worry about," he said, "is tame hogs. Them whut done gone wild. They're not scared of folks, being raised around them and all. They'll light out after you just cause you're there."

"Let's go back home and finish chopping that corn," Timothy said.

"I've got my mind set on marking hogs," Killian said. "And that's what we're gonna do."

Timothy shrugged his shoulders in defeat. He knew there was no changing Killian's mind once he set it to a task. Especially if he thought there was any fun to be had.

"Marking 'em is how we claim them hogs are ours," he said.

"If they ain't marked, they belong to anyone. After we mark 'em, our property's safe. Only a low-class thief would trifle with another man's hogs."

Timothy still seemed to hesitate. Killian would have to talk fast if he was going to keep his younger brother from going back home.

"A man's got to protect his family's property," Killian stood straight and tall. "I intend to put the O'Brien mark on a hog or two 'fore the sun sets today. I'm going to show Papa that I'm a man."

"I'm a man too." Timothy didn't want Killian getting anything on him. "Just how we gonna tell the difference between our regular hogs and them razorbacks?"

"Well, that's the easy part." With his brother recommitted, Killian began to talk as if he was an old hand at marking hogs.

"Regular hogs look just like them that eat slop everday. Round and fat. Mostly colored up white with black spots. That or colored orange like a punkin. Razorbacks are a different animal all together. Kinda dark-colored, nearly black. And they's long and lean." Scrunching up his face and wrinkling his nose, Killian used his right hand to make a pulling motion at his nose, as if to elongate it. "They's got long narrow snouts," he said. "Papa calls 'em *third-row rooters*." He made a snorting sound and Timothy couldn't help but laugh.

"Yeah," Timothy said. "Papa says they can stick their nose through a fence and root up taters in the third row."

Both boys laughed again and started running down the road. The gloom of doubt quickly vanished in the light of laughter.

33

Further down the road Killian stopped, reached
down, and picked up a small stone. "See that hole up
there in that tree?" he said. "Watch me hit it."

"Betcha cain't."

Killian threw the rock, striking just to the left of the
hole.

"Knew you couldn't," Timothy said.

"Let's see you do better," Killian challenged his
younger brother.

For the next few minutes, they took turns trying to hit
the hole. They both came close many times. Finally,
Timothy got one inside the hole.

"Luck," Killian said.

"Papa says luck is sometimes better than skill,"
Timothy grinned.

Killian agreed that it was probably so. Picking up the
horse's reins, he struck out down the road. Timothy was
close behind, while Blue trotted alongside. Soon they
reached the spot where Cliffy Creek entered Little Piney.

Once in the Little Piney bottoms, the boys wasted no
time. Wild hogs were plentiful, and there were lots of
young shoats this year. Every mud hole was littered with
pointed tracks. In a matter of minutes, Blue had trailed up
a large litter, rushed in and scattered them. The
underbrush was alive with young pigs trying to get back
together.

Blue singled out a young shoat, ran it down, grabbed it by the ear and held on for dear life. The pig became quiet and docile with Blue attached to its ear. Killian stepped in quickly and neatly cut a notch in the opposite ear.

On command, Blue released the young pig. It went running off into the bushes and Blue immediately began searching for another. This was going to be easier than Killian had thought.

It was important to single out the young shoats. The idea was to get them away from the rest of the herd. Even the bravest of dogs couldn't handle a herd of mature hogs. If caught by the whole herd, a dog would be quickly cut to shreds by their sharp tusks.

Blue was a smart hog dog. A Catahoula cur, he was fierce to strangers, but dedicated to the protection of his own family. He loved to fight and especially seemed to enjoy fighting hogs. With one blue eye and one brown, ol' Blue was as good with hogs as they get.

In short order, Blue had another fat, young shoat singled out. He rushed in and caught the pig by his left ear. Killian and Timothy rushed to the scene.

Killian handed his younger brother the shotgun as he once again slid the marking knife from its sheath. He had watched his papa mark hogs enough to know how it was done. A quick hand and a sharp knife and this handsome young boar would soon be carrying the O'Brien mark just like its littermate.

The pig was squealing like someone was cutting his throat instead of his ear. Killian was sitting astride the pig helping Blue hold it down while he marked it. Each time the pig struggled to get away, Blue would bear down harder and rumble a throaty growl.

Killian notched the right ear. But this pig didn't want to cooperate. Every time Killian tried to dismount from the pigs back, it would start to wriggle and tug, making it impossible for him to get off. Killian was still trying to find a simple way to release the pig when a huge sow boiled out of the brush.

As soon as the young pig saw his mother, he began to squeal louder than ever. The enraged sow started popping her six-inch tusks with a sound like rifle shots. It was clear she intended to protect her offspring against all comers.

"Watch out!" shouted Timothy.

The sow charged. Her first target was the animal biting at her baby's ear. Blue couldn't turn loose of the pig while Killian was still astride its back. Unable to protect himself or to get away, Blue took the full impact of the first charge.

The sow's knife-like tusks sliced a nasty gash in Blue's hind leg and knocked him to the ground. Blood spurted, spraying the side of the sow's head and the surrounding bushes.

Blue struggled to rise to face the threat. Blood gushed from the wound and his leg collapsed under him. Blue fell back in a heap.

The maddened sow traveled just a few feet past Blue before planting her front feet and wheeling around in a tight circle. She first eyed Blue. Seeing he was no longer an immediate threat, she turned her attention to the human thing riding her offspring.

Muscles bunched in her shoulders as she prepared for her second charge. She pawed at the ground, throwing leaves, twigs, and dirt. Her nostrils flared red.

Once she uncoiled those spring-like red legs, she would be on Killian in seconds. It was going to be a race to see if she could get to him before he could release the shoat and climb a tree.

"Run, Killian! Run!" screamed Timothy.

But Killian froze. He couldn't will his legs to move. All he could do was stare at the sow's ivory tusks glistening wetly in the dappled light. They weren't wet from saliva, they dripped with Blue's blood.

Amidst the clamor of the barking dog, Timothy's screaming, a squealing pig, and a grunting sow, Killian's body was paralyzed in panic. Everything moved in slow motion. With a banshee squeal, the sow unwound and charged.

As she reached Killian, the cacophony was overpowered by the explosion of the shotgun.

34

A numbed silence smothered everything. Time stood still. The sun stopped its steady march across the blue sky. The earth stopped spinning. Every living creature forgot how to breathe. Even the wind failed to stir the leaves in the upper reaches of the tall sycamore. Nothing moved.

An eternity passed before life took another gasp and decided to continue.

The first to move was a slight breeze. Then, a crow caw-cawed from the top of a nearby pine. A sparrow landed on a nearby branch, twisting its head back and forth surveying the scene.

The tangle of honeysuckle quivered where the sow had collapsed. She lay dying, her blood and breath leaking away. Blue struggled to stay on his feet, the ugly gash in his hip dripping blood.

Timothy struggled upright, brushing the seat of his pants. The shotgun lay on the ground beside him. Killian finally figured out how to open his hands, releasing the young pig. It shot away into the brush, glad to make its escape from the sharp knife.

While Killian had frozen before the sow's charge, luckily, Timothy hadn't. As the sow made her first pass, injuring Blue, he'd cocked both hammers of the shotgun. When the sow spun and was ready to make her second charge, he was ready.

He pulled both triggers, giving her a double load of buckshot squarely in the right shoulder. The impact had blown the sow sideways into the honeysuckle and had knocked Timothy on his backside.

"Are you okay?" Timothy asked Killian.

"Uh...yeah...I think so."

"She didn't get you, did she?"

"No."

Killian looked down at his legs and arms. A quick survey revealed that he was indeed still intact. He then turned his attention to Blue. "But she shore got Blue."

"What'll we do?" Timothy was once again the younger brother.

"Hush!" Killian struggled to collect his thoughts. "Let me think." His mind was a swirl of what had just happened, what could have happened, what didn't happen, and what might still happen. It had all taken place so fast he couldn't grasp it all.

"What you think Papa would do?" Timothy asked.

"Look at Blue, he's bleeding something fierce."

Now that it was over, the adrenaline rush had both boys shaking uncontrollably. Timothy was on the verge of tears.

"Here, get your shirt off," Killian ordered.

A plan began to form in his mind. Something he had seen before. "We'll bind Blue up as best we can," he said. "Gather up all the spider web we can find, to staunch the bleeding. We'll have to use both our shirts."

Killian was already taking off his own shirt. He pitched it to Timothy then turned to cut down a sapling. "Then we'll make a *travois* to carry him on," Killian said. "Once we get him home, we can sew him up."

Timothy picked up a broken limb off the ground. He started searching rotten stump holes and under low hanging bushes, looking for spider webs. As he found them, he twirled them onto the stick, then brought the web covered stick back to Killian.

Killian pulled the sticky webs off and gently placed them on the gashes on Blue's hip. Then he wrapped the hound's thigh with his shirt.

"You put pressure on them cuts with your shirt," he told Timothy. "I'll build the travois."

Killian cut two long saplings. With the harness, he attached one end of the poles to the mare's neck and shoulders. With the long ends of the poles dragging the ground behind the mare, he cut more saplings and built a platform near the ground end of the longer poles. On top, the two boys placed Blue.

Killian had seen Indians use this type of transportation numerous times. If Indians could move villages this way, then they could get Blue home. He patted Blue gently on the head.

"What we going to do about the hog?" Timothy asked. It was only then that they noticed the marks on the sow's ears.

"Oh! Hell!" Killian kicked the ground with his bare foot. "She belongs to old man Ranklin."

"Ol' Ben is going to be mad as a wet hen, sure enough." Timothy began. "I heard Papa say that ol' Ben has already lost three or four hogs to poachers. He'll see red when he finds this'un dead."

"Well, it's a cinch we can't un-kill her."

"So," Timothy was on the verge of crying. "What are we gonna do?"

"The hog is already dead, right?"

"Yeah?"

"And it weren't our fault." Killian glanced around nervously.

"Ol' man Ranklin might not see it that way," Timothy rubbed his hands on his thighs.

"We wuz just protecting ourselves," Killian shouted. "A growed man would have done the same."

"Yeah!"

"Anyway," Killian continued. "They ain't nothing we can do to change anything, right?"

"Quit talking in circles," Timothy demanded. "What are we going to do?"

"The way I see it, there's only one thing we can do." Killian had finally made up his mind.

"We'll take her home with us and dress her out. Then we'll put her in the smokehouse, and when Papa gets home, he can get word to old man Ranklin to come and get her."

"You think that best?" Timothy wrung his hands together.

"If'n we leave her here, she's just going to bloat. Won't be any good to anybody," Killian was warming to his decision. "If we take her home, we can at least save the meat. That way old man Ranklin will get some use out of her."

"Sounds okay," Timothy still wasn't convinced.

"And that way, maybe Papa won't be so mad at us either," Killian said.

"Maybe," Timothy said. "But I bet we still get a switching."

Timothy shuddered at the prospect of having to explain all of this to his Papa. To top it off, they hadn't finished hoeing the corn like they were supposed to. A good switching would be welcome compared to what their punishment might be.

It took the boys nearly twenty minutes to get the hog rolled onto the travois beside Blue. The smell of blood made the mare skittish and the sow was bigger than either of the boys. After much tugging and shoving, they were ready and headed home. The ends of the travois left a clear trail where the poles clawed at the ground.

35

Benjamin Ranklin was missing hogs. Four so far. He hadn't seen them in Little Piney bottoms for quite some time. He'd asked around, and nobody else had seen them either. They might have wandered off, but more likely he had a poacher on his hands.

"I think somebody's poaching our hogs," he told his son. "Let's go get your uncle and see what we can find."

"Don't I need a gun, Pa?" the thirteen-year-old Caleb asked.

"Jacob and I will have guns enough," Benjamin said. "You just come along. Be a good chance to teach you how to read sign."

Father and son made their way down Devil's Fork to Jacob's run-down cabin. It was evident that Jacob hadn't been wasting his time making improvements. The cabin was in worse shape than when he'd taken over the place from Benjamin.

"Come go with us," Benjamin said.

"Where to?" he asked.

The older Ranklin explained that he thought someone was poaching his hogs.

"Need to discover the truth of the matter," he said. "See if we can cut some sign. If they're being poached, I'm gonna put a stop to it. If not, I need to know where they're getting off to."

"Has it got to be today?" Jacob asked.

"What you mean?" Benjamin asked. "Does it have to be today."

"Just that another day would be better for me."

"What you got going on today that's so important?" Benjamin demanded.

"Didn't say it was more important," Jacob whined. "Just said another day would be better."

"Suit yourself," Benjamin glared. "You ain't *got* to go. Just thought you might want to help."

Jacob frowned. There was no way he was going to tell his big brother that it was him who was killing his brother's hogs. Nor that he was selling the meat to a tavern over in Scotia. And he hadn't just been killing Benjamin's hogs anyway. He took whatever hogs he came across. Once he cut their ears off, that tavern owner couldn't tell who they had once belonged to. The money was good and there weren't many buffalo or elk around anymore.

No sense in admitting his recent business enterprise. His older brother would probably demand a split of the money. Hell, he might even demand it all. They were his hogs after all.

"Guess I'll stay here then," Jacob said.

"You're sure acting strange," Benjamin said. "Is there something you ain't telling me."

"What you accusing me of?" Jacob blushed.

"Ain't accused you of nothing," Benjamin said. "You're just acting guilty about something."

"Go to hell," Jacob sputtered.

"Something ain't right," Benjamin said. "But I ain't got time to mess with you right now. We'll talk about this later."

"Suit yourself," Jacob turned and walked back inside the cabin.

"Let's go, Caleb," Benjamin said. "Best deal with one situation at a time."

Benjamin and Caleb struck out down the trail for Little Piney bottoms. While on the trail, Caleb had problems keeping up with his father's long strides. Once in the bottoms, Benjamin's gait changed.

Moving through the woods, he would take one or two steps and then stop, slowly surveying everything in sight before taking another well-placed step or two. Then he would repeat the process. Few things escaped his prying eyes.

He showed his son a squirrel lying on a hickory limb, just its ears and one eye visible above the curve of the limb.

"Don't do no good looking for a whole animal," he told his son. "Won't never see much that way. You got to look for parts."

Caleb was doing a fine job of noticing little things when Benjamin suddenly raised his hand, demanding he stop stock still where he was.

"Look there," Benjamin said. "See all them broke limbs over there?"

After much searching, Caleb saw what his father was pointing out. About twenty feet away, he could see where the leaves had been torn up and limbs the size of a man's little finger littered the ground.

Upon closer inspection, Benjamin pointed out where a scuffle had taken place. They found where saplings had been chopped down. They found where a horse had stood, its circular-shaped tracks plain in the soft soil. They found hog tracks galore. And they found blood.

Benjamin Ranklin read signs as some men might read a newspaper. Everything was as clear to him as if he'd been there when it happened. He pointed out where two people had built a drag to tote off their prize. And that prize was a hog. Probably his hog, if he had his guess.

"Let's follow these drag marks," he said. "Where they stop, we'll find the truth of the matter."

The two started through the woods, following the drag marks in the soft ground. The drag marks could have been followed by a blind man. Whoever it was wasn't trying to hide their tracks.

36

Once home, the O'Brien boys went straight into the barn, pulling the travois into the cool passageway.

Josephine had heard them coming and was standing on the front porch watching.

"Joe," Killian called out. "Bring me a needle for sewing."

Josephine skipped out to where the two brothers were busy with something they'd drug in behind the mare. Upon entering the shadow of the barn passageway, she stopped dead in her tracks at the sight of blood.

"What on earth," she said.

"Never mind about that," Killian said. "Fetch me a sewing needle."

"What's wrong with Blue?" Joe asked.

"He's hurt," Killian was losing his patience. "Fetch me the needle like I said."

"But what are you going to do?" she asked.

"Blue's been cut up by this sow," Killian said. "We gotta get him sewed up."

"You stick him with a needle," Joe said, "He'll bite you."

"No, he won't." Killian hoped what he was saying was true. Blue might bite him, but he would have to try.

"I've seen Papa sew him up before. He'll be okay. Now fetch that needle like I said."

Josephine shook her head before heading back toward the house at a run.

"Timothy," Killian said. "Let's get Blue off the travois. That mare ain't gonna stand still and I don't want Blue moving when I'm trying to sew him up. Make him a pallet of hay, we'll put him on that."

Blue whined a little in protest at being moved but settled quickly once on the pallet. His mismatched eyes showed pain, but they also showed trust.

"Now, get me a long horsehair from the mare's tail," Killian said. "We'll use that for thread."

Josephine returned with the needle and Killian threaded it with the horsehair Timothy had pulled. Then he turned to Blue who was still lying on the travois.

"I know I ain't Pa," he said. "But I'll do the best I can."

Blue laid his head down as if to say, 'go ahead' but Josephine climbed into the loft.

"Where you going?" Timothy asked.

"You two are not Papa," she said. "If Blue don't take to your doctoring, I'm not gonna be in range of those teeth. I'll watch from up here thank you very much, and I'll tell Papa how you got dog bit."

"Dog bit or not," Killian said. "We owe it to Blue."

Killian did a fair job with what little skill he obtained. Blue, for his part, whined only a couple of times, putting his trust in the young O'Brien. Fifteen minutes later, the job was finished.

"Joe," Killian asked, "do you think you could climb down here now and fetch Blue some water? He's not gonna bite now."

"I was hoping he'd bite you both," she said as she climbed down.

"Very funny," Killian said. "Now we got to try and save that hog meat."

Timothy got the block and tackle from the barn and hung it in the large cedar tree. They led the mare underneath, stuck the long gambrel between the hog's hind legs, and pulled her up off the ground. The gambrel, a long wooden rod used to spread the hog's hind legs apart, was used so the dressing process could be accomplished. Once the hog was in the air, they took the travois off the mare and turned her loose into the corral with a pat on her flank.

"Would you mind giving her a portion of oats," Killian asked Joe. "She's done a good day's work."

Timothy had gone to the house and brought back the good skinning knives. The two boys jumped into the task at hand. Splitting the sow down her belly, from tail to neck, her guts plopped out on the ground with a wet smack.

"Need to get her opened up, so she can cool down and bleed out," Killian said.

"I'll get a sheet to cover her so blowflies won't get to the meat and lay their eggs," Josephine offered.

As they went about their task of saving the meat, Josephine asked question after question about their adventure. The two told her a story mixed with fear and bravado. Timothy embellished only slightly the part of him saving his older brother from the sow. Josephine made them tell her the story three times before she lost interest in them and the hog.

When through, the boys went to check on Blue and Josephine headed back up to the house.

Killian and Timothy were focused entirely on the medical attention aimed at Blue. Only Josephine, sitting on the front porch, noticed Benjamin Ranklin and his son Caleb slip into the yard. The Ranklin's had followed the deep travois drag marks from Cliffy Creek bottoms, straight to the O'Brien's yard. It hadn't taken much woodcraft to do so.

Benjamin treaded quietly up to the hog hanging in the cedar tree. The ears sticking out from under the sheet left no doubt as to whose property it was. He came to a quick, although incorrect conclusion. He'd finally caught the low life's who were fattening up on pork, at his expense. Now they'd pay the fiddler.

Killian was intent on inspecting his handy work. As gently as he could, he was using a wet rag to soak the dried blood from Blue's wound. Timothy was watching over his shoulder when Blue began to bristle. A throaty growl began to bubble from deep inside his chest.

"Easy boy," Killian said, thinking the dog was growling at him. "Rest."

"Trash!"

Benjamin Ranklin's sudden exclamation reverberated like thunder. "Kill my brood sow," he shouted. "And think you'd get away with it?"

Startled, Timothy instinctively grabbed for the shotgun leaning against the barn door. Just as his fingers touched its wooden forearm, Benjamin Ranklin shot him in the back.

Timothy spun once and fell facedown. The bullet struck him dead center, ending his life instantly. Blood quickly painted the ground around him.

"No!" Killian screamed and grabbed for the falling gun.

Caleb Ranklin moved quicker. When coming across the yard, he'd picked up a stick of firewood. Now he swung it like a club. The blow struck Killian alongside the head, near the temple. He collapsed, unconscious.

Blue tried valiantly to rise to protect the boys. Benjamin Ranklin snatched the stick from Caleb, swinging it with all his might. It made a sweeping arch up and then down fast, striking Blue's head. Blue's life ended with a sickening crunch.

Josephine witnessed everything from her position on the porch. Her eyes couldn't believe what they were seeing. The quickness and brutality of it all froze her voice in her throat. She couldn't move. Her mouth was open, screaming. But nothing was coming out. She fainted.

37

It was dark when Josephine awoke to the sound of trace chains clinking. Patrick and Connell were returning from a day of building to find a world destroyed.

Timothy and Blue were both dead.

Killian was conscious, but he was talking out of his head.

It took hours before Patrick could make any sense of what had happened. Josephine couldn't wrap her mind around it. Surely it was just a bad dream. She couldn't remember everything that had happened. What she could remember was too incredible.

Timothy was gone—Killian was on death's doorstep.

It had all happened so fast. Or had it happened at all?

Patrick had her tell and re-tell everything she could remember. She remembered the story the boys had told her about the sow. She remembered Benjamin Ranklin's suddenly appearing as if from nowhere, surprising everyone.

In her mind, she could see Timothy reaching for the shotgun. Everything moving in slow motion. Just as his fingers touched it, there had been that awful blast.

Smoke and fire billowed from where Benjamin Ranklin was standing. It reached out and licked at Timothy's back. She could see him spin and collapse. Then everything turned red, then black. That was all she could remember. She couldn't remember anything about what had happened to Killian.

The hog was gone, but it was evident it had been there. The rope still dangled from the cedar tree and bottle flies worked the gut pile. The travois the brothers had made was gone. Probably used by the murderer to reclaim the hog.

There were tracks in the sandy ground of the yard. One set were those of a grown man, the others were of someone smaller. With what Josephine could remember and what Patrick could observe, the conclusion was simple.

Benjamin Ranklin had murdered his twelve-year-old son in cold blood. From the looks of things, Killian might soon join his brother and Helen.

38

The wake for young Timothy lasted two days. He was buried in the family plot next to Helen. Patrick read a passage from the Bible about the resurrection, then dropped to one knee and sprinkled dirt into the grave.

"There's no love greater than that of a mother," Patrick's voice cracked.

His face was ashen and puffy; his eyes swollen and blood-shot. He had wept so much that his eyes contained no more moisture they could release. He rose shakily to his feet, and with bowed body and spirit continued.

"For now," Patrick said. "I'll be leaving you in your mother's care." Turning his face to heaven he said, "May God hold you both in the hollow of His hand."

Then he turned and walked away from the grave. It had been hard enough losing three children back in New York. But then he'd been able to share the pain with Helen. Together they'd suffered their losses by leaning heavily on each other.

Then he'd lost his green-eyed angel seven years ago. Now he would have to find the way for a parent to lose a child alone.

Losing three children to disease had been hard, but this was different. Disease doesn't have a face. A murderer does. Benjamin Ranklin had viciously taken Timothy's life. As long as he breathed the same air as the rest of the world, that face would haunt Patrick. Every corner of

Cliffy Hollow would taunt him with Benjamin's threats to rid the hollow of O'Briens.

A dangerous look settled on his face. Those friends who dared to look him in the eye saw the dark fire that was only banked for a while. It would blaze again and consume his very soul. This wasn't over.

But Patrick's first responsibility was to those still living. He had to shoulder the task of mending his broken family. As in the past, he reached out to his good friends, Elizabeth and Hans Göbel.

Elizabeth came to stay with them for a couple of weeks. She was able to nurse Killian back to health from his fever, but his mind didn't improve.

"Poor, sweet Killian will never be the same," she told Patrick. "That blow to the head has addled him for life."

"I still don't understand the why of it all," Patrick shook his head.

"Joe doesn't even remember how Killian came to harm. The last she remembers is Timothy being murdered."

"Somehow that boy of Ben's was involved," Hans said. "Of that, you can be sure."

"It was probably his tracks I found along with Ranklin's," Patrick agreed.

"Yes, I've known he was a bad seed," Elizabeth added, "ever since he was born."

"A hell-wolf spawned by the old he-wolf himself," Hans spit the words.

Patrick gave them both a questioning look. "What are you talking about?"

"Don't you remember?" Elizabeth tried to explain. "As Killian was born in the light of the meteor shower, that boy was born in the dark of an eclipse. Marked with the cloven hoof of a satyr. There's a curse on that lad. Only bad things will ever come of him."

Elizabeth seemed to think that was explanation enough, but Patrick still didn't get it. Anyway, Caleb was not his concern right now. He had buried a son and now he must protect his family from further harm.

Cursed or not, Caleb wasn't much more than a boy himself. The real devil in all this would have to be held accountable. That devil had black eyes and grinned from behind a bearded face.

"What are we going to do about Josephine?" Elizabeth asked.

"I don't want this discussed any further in front of her," there was steel in Patrick's voice. "That baby girl has been through enough. She don't even remember anyone other than Benjamin Ranklin being here. I'd just as soon she forget it all."

"Let's take a walk," Hans said.

Patrick blindly followed Hans down to the mill. Neither man spoke, both lost in their own hell. When they reached the millrace, Hans reached in the familiar spot and pulled the brown jug from the cool water. Lifting it to his lips, he took a long swallow. Then he offered it to Patrick.

"No thanks," Patrick said. "I've got to keep my head about me."

"I can see in your Irish heart, what you plan to do," Hans said. "Few in this valley will blame you for the way you feel."

"Blame or not," Patrick said. "Timothy's blood calls me."

"The Ranklin's will be expecting something from you," Hans said. "They'll be watching."

"If they're watching," Patrick said. "Then they'll see it when it comes."

"You want me to take care of this, yah?" Hans offered. "Benjamin won't be expecting it from me. All you need do is ask."

"Thanks, Hans," Patrick assured his friend. "I'll be taking care of this myself. It's the wearer who knows best where the shoe pinches."

"There's something else you don't know," Hans said. "Didn't think it proper to tell you before now."

"Tell me what?"

39

Seven years had been a long time for Hans to keep his secret. A secret based on suspicions that would only cause trouble if not true. If his conclusions were wrong, he would have brought hurt to more than just his friend.

"Back when Helen died in that cabin fire," Hans began. "Black-Fox did a little looking around after things settled down. He brought me a tomahawk he found in the bushes behind the cabin."

"Lots of tomahawks in this country," Patrick didn't get the connection. "You mean an Indian tomahawk?"

"Kinda," Hans said. "There was something a little different about this particular tomahawk."

"Different how?"

"This one had two rows of brass tacks nailed down each side," Hans said. "The Osage liked to decorate their tomahawks that way."

"There haven't been any Osage around here in years," Patrick said. "Does Black-Fox think Indians had something to do with the fire?"

"Not exactly," Hans said. "But maybe somebody associated with them."

"Benjamin Ranklin traded with the Indians!" Patrick leaped ahead in Han's story.

"Osage to be exact," added Hans.

The wheels were turning rapidly in Patrick's mind. Everyone, at one time or another had been forced to hear Benjamin Ranklin brag about his earlier exploits. He'd been an employee of the St. Louis Fur Trading Company, back when this was all part of the Louisiana Territory.

233

He'd even discovered the Little Piney valley while trading with the Osage.

"Both Benjamin and Jacob Ranklin had a tomahawk like the one Black-Fox found," Hans said. "Always kept 'em tucked in their belts. Benjamin used to trade tomahawks like that to the Osage."

"That's right."

"Ain't seen Benjamin or Jacob either one toting one since the fire," Hans said.

"Black-Fox think it was the Ranklin's?"

"Said there were signs made by two big men around the outside of the cabin," Hans said. "Signs where they built a fire and made up some torches with pine heartwood. He thinks they torched the house with Helen inside. Found the tomahawk nearby. They probably dropped in their haste to get away."

"Why didn't you tell me this before?" Patrick demanded.

"Only speculation," Hans said. "Nothing that would hold up in a court."

"The Ranklin's will never see a court," Patrick swore. "Revenge will be mine!"

Over the next couple of months, not much happened. People had warned Benjamin Ranklin of what he already knew. He should expect some sort of retribution from Patrick O'Brien.

His brother Jacob felt the heat too. He left his wife and kids to tend the house place, and he lit out for Spadra Landing. He was going to take a business trip up to Fort Smith. Jacob told Priscilla he should be back in a couple of months.

Benjamin wasn't about to run away. Not when he had already rid Cliffy Hollow of two O'Briens. If Patrick came looking for him, he would have the chance to bury another. With nothing left in his way but children, he could reclaim his hollow.

The mountain man knew the side of being hunted from his early days in the Purchase. To be on the safe side, he carried a gun everywhere he went. Even to the privy. He stayed close to home, not venturing far from the familiar. He'd learned from fighting Indians, it was best to have your enemy come to you. He was confident he'd be ready if that damn Irishman tried anything. He'd managed to keep his hair in worse situations.

Someone got word to Patrick that Jacob had high-tailed it out of the country. That was all right. He stood a better chance of catching them alone if they were separated. His plan required patience. All he had to do was bide his time. Eventually, they would lose their initial fear of retribution and drop their guard. When they did, he'd be there.

He watched Benjamin in secret, using skills Black-Fox had taught him so he wouldn't be observed. He waited for him to settle back into his normal routine. As time passed, with no confrontation coming from Patrick, Benjamin Ranklin became confident again. After a few weeks of watching, Patrick figured the best time to catch Benjamin alone would be on a Sunday morning.

Ranklin had a habit of riding to church alone, ahead of his wife and son. They would come later, in a wagon. Sarah and Caleb usually stopped and picked up Jacob's wife and children.

Benjamin didn't attend the services himself. No need for him to be found inside. Rarely did he darken the doors of the church, except for a wedding or a funeral. He left the religion stuff to the women and children. Instead, he liked to get there early and visit with the menfolk out in the wagon yard. They'd sit around outside, smoking, laughing, and telling tall tales. It was a time to catch up on all the local gossip and to brag on how much the valley owed him.

While the sanctified were occupied inside, singing hymns, one of the backsliders would sneak out a jug. It was rough mountain mash, and it burned going down—but it got the job done.

On one of those tongue loosening occasions, Benjamin Ranklin had bragged a little too much about how the valley owed his family.

"Ya'll owe me and mine more than you know!" he'd said.

"You mean that old story about you being the first to lay eyes on this valley?" one of the men laughed. "That was a long time ago, Ben."

"There's stories you've all heard, true enough," Benjamin winked. "Then there's stories you don't hear."

"What kind of stories?"

"Stories of ridding the valley of pox and poachers," Benjamin lowered his voice. "Was it one of you lily-livered saps whut put a stop to trash poaching our livestock?"

When no one answered, Benjamin took the silence as a chance to shame his audience even more with their lack of civic pride or action.

"Who was it stopped the spread of pox in this valley?" he asked. "Who burnt it out cabin by cabin? Any of you got the gumption to do something like that?"

"What are you talking about, Ben?" one asked. "I'm not following what you're saying."

"There was only one cabin that burned during that time," another observed.

"I've said enough already." He wiped his piggish mouth with the back of his hand. "There some things people don't need to know all the details of. They should just appreciate what's done fer 'em. That's all I'm saying."

There was little doubt that Ben had killed young Timothy O'Brien, and his son Caleb had addled the younger Killian. The gossips already knew that accusation, and few doubted it to be true. This morning, he was all but admitting it. He was saying it was 'him who'd *cleaned out* the poachers'.

It was common knowledge to anyone who'd ever sat in on one of these church side conversations, that he had a low opinion of anyone named O'Brien. But here he was making admissions they had never heard before.

If what he was saying was true, he was admitting to burning down the cabin on Gobblers Point. That was where Helen O'Brien had died along with that immigrant family. Was he admitting to murdering two O'Brien's?

Word of Ranklin's boastful claims quickly got back to Patrick. It was not an admission of guilt, true enough, but it confirmed his suspicions. It was time to end it.

It was cool that October morning in 1847. It had been a clear, still night with a waning moon. The morning held just a hint of frost. Chill bumps formed on Patrick's upper arms as he waited for the intended rendezvous.

Motion caught his eye, but it was just dry leaves being chased across the trail by short gusts of wind wanting to play. Or maybe they were sweeping the path to hell clean. The early morning sun climbed above the treetops, struggling to wash the air with a warm golden tint. Nearby Devil's Fork bubbled over the rocks, mumbling a conversation to no one in particular.

Golds, yellows, oranges, and reds would soon set the hillsides ablaze as the sun took hold of the day. On any other morning, the world would have seemed vibrant and alive. But today Death waited under the black walnut's spreading limbs with Patrick. The dark specter whispered its sweet promise of revenge. Once the deed was accomplished, all would be repaired.

Patrick had set his ambush well. He'd selected a level spot along Devil's Fork Trail, the only one Ranklin would use from his home place to Little Piney. On one side of the trail was Devil's Fork creek itself. On the opposite side of the trail was a rock wall. It went straight up for twenty feet. There would be no escape in that direction. The spot was near the junction with the main road, but it was a good distance from either Ranklin cabin.

It was far enough off the main Little Piney road that it would reduce the chance of another traveler interrupting. Patrick didn't want intruders stumbling upon his meeting with Benjamin Ranklin before he had accomplished his goal.

The sound of horse hooves striking rock warned of Benjamin's approach. When he was within ten yards,

Patrick stepped from behind the tree, facing his antagonist.

"Benjamin Lyle Ranklin!" he called. "Revenge is mine!"

Benjamin pulled back on the reins of his appaloosa. The horse stopped in the middle of the trail.

"You thought you'd be going to church this morning," Patrick called out. Flint sparked his voice and the fire of redemption consumed his eyes. "Instead," Patrick said. "You'll be going to hell."

Patrick brought the rifle to his shoulder and squeezed the trigger just as Benjamin Ranklin tried to rein the appaloosa around. The sudden sawing on the reins caused the horse to rear up. The horse's movement spoiled Patrick's aim. Instead of punching a hole in his chest, the bullet struck Ranklin in the neck.

Tumbling out of the saddle, Ranklin fell backward into the dust of the road. Trying vainly to rise, he fell back again, clutching at his throat. Blood and air mixed as they bubbled out of the nasty wound.

He tried to cuss, but all that came out was a gurgling sound. Rolling over and over, he tried desperately to rise to his feet. Dark streams of blood spurted from between his fingers. Writhing and twisting, his body came to rest against a holly tree at the side of the road.

Patrick crossed the trail and knelt on one knee next to him. Looking into his tortured face, he leaned close to ensure Benjamin Ranklin heard his final message.

"You have murdered your last O'Brien," Patrick said.

Benjamin Ranklin gurgled an unintelligible response. Patrick leaned closer as Benjamin tried again.

"Caleb..." His last breath carried the single word as his body went limp. Benjamin Ranklin was dead.

Patrick felt neither regret nor remorse. The death was something that had to be done, like killing rats in the corn crib. But Benjamin Ranklin's murder carried a price.

As Patrick watched the light fade from Ranklin's black eyes, his own brown eyes darkened too. Their spark of life slowly dissolved into a dull luster. His didn't glaze over with the specter of death like Ranklin's had they simply exposed the death of his soul.

When Patrick had first come to this land, he'd been concerned about the possibility of having to pay for his folly. Instead, others had paid. Helen, Killian, and now Benjamin Ranklin. Someone always had to pay; it was as simple as that. But in the end, maybe he had paid the most.

With slumped shoulders, a much older Patrick O'Brien rose and walked away. The feud with the Ranklin's was not over. Only a fool would have thought that. But Patrick's soul could no longer carry it. If revenge demanded a hearing with another Ranklin—then that duty would fall to another O'Brien.

Patrick returned to Cliffy Hollow. He returned to days spent mending a wounded family. Returned to twilights shared with his loving Helen. Returned to nights visited by ghosts whispering the name...Caleb.